George A. Macfarren

The Rudiments of Harmony

with progressive exercises and appendix

George A. Macfarren

The Rudiments of Harmony
with progressive exercises and appendix

ISBN/EAN: 9783337387495

Printed in Europe, USA, Canada, Australia, Japan

Cover: Foto ©Andreas Hilbeck / pixelio.de

More available books at **www.hansebooks.com**

THE

RUDIMENTS OF HARMONY,

WITH

PROGRESSIVE EXERCISES AND APPENDIX.

BY

G. A. MACFARREN.

SEVENTEENTH AND REVISED EDITION.

LONDON:

J. B. CRAMER AND CO., 201, REGENT STREET, W.

PRICE FIVE SHILLINGS.

In Paper Cover, 4s.

1888.

LONDON :

SWIFT AND CO., TYPE-MUSIC AND GENERAL PRINTERS,

NEWTON STREET, HIGH HOLBORN, W.C.

PREFACE.

This book presents the truth, and nothing but the truth, though not the whole truth, on the boundless subject of which it treats.

It is designed for the use of beginners in the study, and its object is fully and clearly to explain such points as come under daily experience, while it discusses slightly some others which are less frequently exemplified in composition.

Being addressed to beginners, its explanations are all dogmatical; no arguments are advanced to justify any views of the subject which are set forth since such a style of teaching would perplex the unpractised attention of a pupil and ample vindication of all that is here stated is to be found in books fitted rather for studied musicians than for mere learners. The book contains nothing new in theory;*but it differs in arrangement from works that have already appeared, according as practice has led me to differ in teaching, from the course pursued in any of these works; its chief pretensions are in the endeavour to state first principles distinctly, and to remove discrepancies between the laws of early theorists and the practice of modern composers.

To facilitate reference, each chapter contains all that is said upon the branch of the subject therein treated; though the course of study will render it necessary to pass to some later chapters before concluding earlier ones. Thus, in the chapter on Intervals, it is not desirable to read of Intervals beyond the Octave, until the student have advanced to the chapter on Suspensions, in which the employment of the interval of the 9th is first noticed;—in the chapter on Keys and Scales, it is not desirable to read of the Minor Key until the Student have written exercises of common chords in the Major Key; or to read of the chromatic scale, until he have advanced to the treatment of chromatic chords; &c. The order in which the book should first be read, is indicated in the Table of Contents, where the several divisions of the subject are progressively ranged according to the succession in which they should be studied.

It is eminently desirable that the student should construct his own exercises; however, for the sake of those to whom this is too difficult a task, and as models for those who are able to undertake it, a series of Progressive Exercises on every division of the subject is here furnished, which, like the Table of Contents, indicates the order in which the several divisions of the subject should be studied.

* The distinction of the strict from the free style of harmony, and the explanation of the entire chromatic system, were first made by the late Alfred Day.

June, 1860.

TABLE OF CONTENTS,

INDICATING THE ORDER IN WHICH THE SEVERAL DIVISIONS OF THE SUBJECT SHOULD BE STUDIED.

RUDIMENTS OF HARMONY.

DEFINITIONS.

SECTION 1. *Melody.* Notes in succession.*

2. *Harmony.* Notes in combination.

3. *Counterpoint.* A melody that accompanies another melody. Counterpoint is simple, when the several melodies proceed note against note with each other; it is florid, when one melody proceeds in shorter notes than the other, and the independence of the two is thus more clearly marked; it is double, when the two melodies may change their relative position, the higher being placed below the lower, or the lower above the higher.

4. *Score.* The several parts of the harmony, each on a separate staff, ranged one above the other on the same page.

5. *Bass.* The lowest note in any harmonic combination, however high or however low the entire combination may be.

6. *Chord.* Two or more notes sounded together.

7. *Root.* The note from which a chord is derived, and after which such chord is named.

8. *Triad.* A bass with its 3rd and 5th, whatever the qualities of these intervals: whether the 3rd be major or minor; whether the 5th be perfect, augmented, or diminished.

9. *Arpeggio.* The notes of a chord sounded successively by a single part, instead of sounded together by several parts.

10. *Modulation.* Passing from one key to another.

11. *Diatonic.* Consisting of notes according to the signature of the key. The leading note of the minor key, though indicated by an accidental sharp or natural, is diatonic; so also are the major 6th and minor 7th of the arbitrary minor scale. When modulation occurs, the accidentals that denote the change of key are to be regarded as belonging to the signature of the new key, and thus are diatonic in the key to which the modulation is made.

12. *Chromatic.* Consisting of notes indicated by accidentals, which induce no modulation. A note or a chord either belongs to the key of the passage that precedes it, or to the key of the passage that succeeds it; if that which precedes and that which succeeds it be both in the same key, this note or chord, though foreign to the signature, induces no modulation, and is, therefore, chromatic.

13. *Enharmonic.* Consisting of intervals smaller than semitones. On keyed instruments the distinction between two notes of the same sound, but with different names (as C sharp and D flat, E sharp and F), is enharmonic.

---

* This is the broadest technical definition of the term. Conventionally, "a melody" signifies the same as "a tune," and this is bound by the laws of rhythm and other conditions, which, more or less, equally affect harmonic as they do melodic progressions. The poetical acceptation of the words *melody, harmony, concord,* and *discord,* is not to be regarded in their technical employment.

14. *Concord.* A chord that is satisfactory in itself, and may be approached and quitted without consideration of what chord precedes or follows it (Except Chap. IV. sects. 26 to 31).

15. *Discord.* A chord that must be resolved upon another chord, or a note that must be resolved upon another note.

16. *Preparation.* Anticipating the dissonant note by previously sounding it in the same part in which it is to form the discord.

17. *Resolution.* The progression of a discord to the chord which is obliged to follow it, and of the dissonant note to the note in such chord to which it is obliged to proceed.

18. *Diatonic Discords* are formed of notes of the diatonic scale artificially combined; they are common to all the notes of the key. All of these discords, except passing notes, must be prepared, and have one fixed resolution.

19. *Fundamental Discords* are formed of the notes generated according to the natural system of harmonics; they are all derived from the dominant, the supertonic, and the tonic. Those belonging to the last two roots are all chromatic; those belonging to the first root are some chromatic and some diatonic: they require no preparation, and have various resolutions.

20. *Close,* or *Cadence.* The completion of a phrase or rhythmical period. A full close, or perfect cadence, is when a phrase terminates with the common chord of the key-note, preceded by the harmony of the dominant.* A half close is when a phrase terminates on the harmony of the dominant. An interrupted close is when the course of the passage leads to a full close, but breaks away from this;—the conventional form of interrupted close is when a phrase terminates with the common chord of the submediant, preceded by the dominant harmony. Other cadences are in less frequent use, which are not defined by special names. †

21. *The Ancient, Strict,* or *Diatonic Style of Harmony,* admits of diatonic notes only, subjects every note of the scale to the same laws,‡ allows the 4th to the bass to be employed in no way but as a discord, admits of no unprepared discords except passing notes, and allows not passing notes to be approached by leap.

22. *The Modern, Free,* or *Chromatic Style of Harmony,* admits of chromatic as well as diatonic notes, admits of exceptional treatment of certain notes, allows the 4th to the bass to be employed as a concord, admits of fundamental discords, and allows passing notes to be approached by leap.

---

* The plagal cadence, less commonly used, is when the subdominant precedes the key-note in a final close.
† Appendix A.

‡ This may appear contradictory to the prohibition of the employment of the triads on the 3rd and 7th of the key, and other rules in Chapter IV. It is beyond the purpose and the limits of the present book to remove such appearance of contradiction; but, were there space for argument, the rules referred to might be adduced to prove the definition of the strict style to which they may seem to be opposed.

CHAPTER I.

INTERVALS.

Sect. 1. An unison is one note sounded by two or more voices or instruments at the same time.

2. An interval is the distance from one note to another.

3. Intervals are reckoned upwards, except the contrary be specified.

INTERVALS WITHIN THE OCTAVE.

4. A semitone is the interval from any note on the pianoforte to the next note.
A semitone is diatonic (Definitions, sect. 11), when the two notes, between which it lies, bear different names, as from B to C, &c.
A semitone is chromatic (Definitions, sect. 12), when the two notes bear the same name, but are varied by a sharp or a flat; as from C to C sharp, from D flat to D natural.

5. A tone includes two semitones; as from B to C sharp, from C to D.

6. Other intervals are named (according to the *alphabetical* relation of the two notes), 2nds, 3rds, 4ths, 5ths, 6ths, 7ths, and 8ths,—the note from which the interval to another note is reckoned, being regarded as the 1st; thus, from C to D is a 2nd, from C to E is a 3rd, from C to F is a 4th, &c.
These numerical names of intervals depend entirely upon the *alphabetical* names of the notes between which the intervals lie, wholly irrespective of inflection by sharps or flats; thus, from C to D flat, from C to D natural, and from C to D sharp, are all 2nds, while from C to E flat is a 3rd.

7. For all purposes of harmony an interval is still regarded as a 2nd, 3rd, 4th, &c., though it include an octave (8th), or several octaves (8ths) beyond the real notes defined by these numbers; thus, any E above any C is regarded as the 3rd of C, however extreme the distance between these two notes, 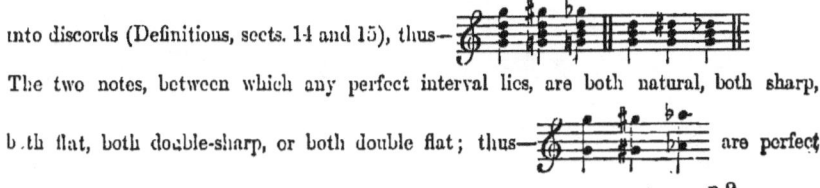 (Chap. I. sect. 16.)

8. There are several qualities of 2nds, 3rds, 4ths, &c.; these, though the notes bear the same *alphabetical* relation, though they stand on the same lines or spaces, are distinguished by the greater or less number of semitones they contain, according as the notes may be sharp, or flat, or natural.

9. The intervals of the 8th, the 5th, and the 4th, are called *perfect*, because they cannot be increased or lessened by sharps or flats, without changing them from concords into discords (Definitions, sects. 14 and 15), thus—

The two notes, between which any perfect interval lies, are both natural, both sharp, both flat, both double-sharp, or both double flat; thus— are perfect

B 2

8ths ;   are perfect 5ths ; and   are perfect 4ths. The single exceptions from this law are with regard to the 5th of B, and its inversion the 4th of F. (*For other distinctions of the perfect intervals, see* Chap. I. sect. 14; Chap. III. sects. 5 to 9; Chap. X. sect. 14.)

10. The intervals of the 3rd and 6th, and the 2nd and 7th, may be increased or lessened, and are, in both forms, alike concords or discords; thus   with a major (or greater) 3rd, and   with a minor (or smaller) 3rd, are both concords ;   a major 2nd, and   a minor 2nd, are both discords.

11. Other 5ths and 4ths, besides the perfect, and other 3rds and 6ths, 2nds and 7ths, besides the major and minor, are also employed in harmony: these are augmented and diminished,—augmented being more than perfect or more than major, and diminished being less than perfect or less than minor,—and they are all discords; thus   being a perfect 5th,   is an augmented 5th, and   is a diminished 5th ;   being a major 6th,   is an augmented 6th; and   being a minor 3rd,   is a diminished 3rd.

INVERSION OF INTERVALS.

12. Inversion of intervals changes the relative position of the two notes by placing the lower above the higher,   or by placing the higher below the lower,

13. The number of any interval within the octave, added to the number of its inversion, makes nine; thus, the inversion of a 2nd is a 7th,—of a 3rd is a 6th,—of a 4th is a 5th, &c.

14. The inversion of a perfect interval produces a perfect interval,   (Chap. I. sect. 9.)

15. With the major and minor, and with the augmented and diminished intervals, and their inversions, however much one division of the octave is greater, just so much is the other division of the octave less;—accordingly, their quality is reversed by their inversion : major produces minor, and minor major; augmented produces diminished, and diminished augmented.

TABLE OF INTERVALS AND THEIR INVERSIONS, STATING THE NUMBER OF SEMITONES IN EACH.

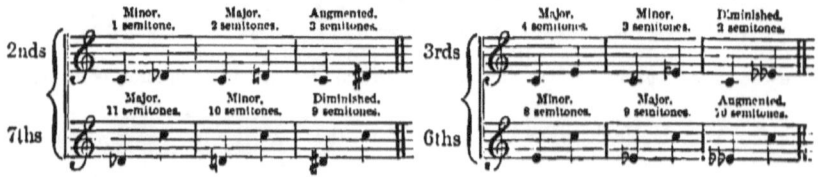

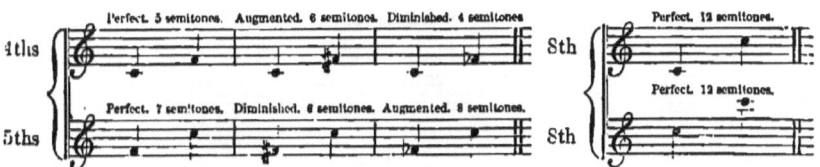

₊ *Be it observed that the number of semitones in any interval, added to the number of semitones in its inversion, always makes the twelve which complete the octave.*

INTERVALS BEYOND THE OCTAVE.

16. The intervals of the 9th, the 11th, and the 13th, are exceptions from the rule given in sect. 7. These are entirely distinct in treatment from the 2nd, the 4th, and the 6th, which are represented by the same notes, and they are used in different combinations.

TABLE OF INTERVALS BEYOND THE OCTAVE.

₊ *In figuring basses, 9 is used when the discord is in an upper part, 2 when the discord is in the bass.*

CHAPTER II.

KEYS AND SCALES.

1. A KEY is a certain arrangement of notes with reference to any one note, which is called the key-note or tonic, and from which the key is named.

2. The 2nd of the key (the note next above the key-note), is called the supertonic; the 3rd of the key, the mediant; the 4th, the subdominant; the 5th, the dominant; the 6th, the submediant; and the 7th, the leading-note.

3. Keys are major and minor.

4. A scale is a gradual succession of notes, ascending or descending.

5. A scale is major or minor, according as the key (of the notes of which it is composed is major or minor.

6. A scale may also be chromatic (Definitions, sect. 12); or some only of the chromatic notes may be interspersed in the major or minor scale.

MAJOR KEY AND SCALE.

7. In the major key, all the intervals from the key-note are either major or perfect; thus, the 2nd and 3rd are major, the 4th and 5th are perfect, and the 6th and 7th are major.

8. These, placed in gradual succession, form the major scale, which has a semitone between the 3rd and 4th, and between the 7th and 8th degrees,—and a tone between every other successive two degrees.

SCALE OF C.

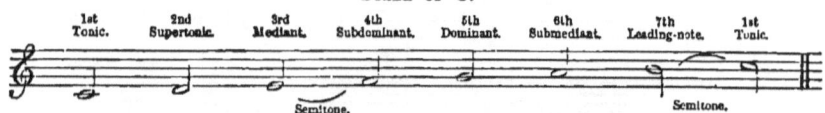

9. Precisely the same arrangement of notes with reference to the key-note, as in the key of C, prevails in every major key; and to induce this, sharps are employed in some keys, and flats in others.

10. When a key has only one sharp, this is F sharp, and each additional sharp is a 5th above (or its inversion, a 4th below) the sharp last added. When all the seven notes have been made sharp, double-sharps are employed; thus, F double-sharp is used in place of an eighth sharp,—and these are successively added in the same order.

11. The sharp last added is the leading-note, which, by this sharp, is made to be a semitone below the key-note, and thus the key-note is always a minor 2nd above it; so, when F sharp is the only sharp, G is the key-note;—when C sharp is added, D is the key-note, &c.

12. When a key has only one flat, this is B flat, and each additional flat is a 5th below (or its inversion a 4th above) the flat last added. When all the seven notes have been made flat, double-flats are employed; thus, B double-flat is used in place of an eighth flat,—and these are added in the same order.

13. The flat last added is the subdominant, which, by this flat, is made to be a semitone above the 3rd of the key, and thus the key-note is always a perfect 4th below it. So, when B flat is the only flat, F is the key-note; when E flat is added, B flat is the key-note, &c.

MINOR KEY AND HARMONIC MINOR SCALE.

14. The minor key has three flats more, or three sharps less in its signature, than the major key of the same note: thus, the key of C having no flats, that of C minor has three; and the key of A having three sharps, that of A minor has none.

15. The leading-note, in the minor key as in the major, is but a semitone below the key-note; to induce this, however, one of the three notes, changed by the signature from the corresponding notes in the major key, is restored by an accidental natural or sharp wherever it occurs: but, though raised by an accidental natural or sharp, the leading-note in the minor key is still diatonic. (Definitions, sect. 11.)

16. There are, then, two notes in the minor key different from the notes of the corresponding degrees of the major key; these are the 3rd and 6th, which, by the change of signature, are made minor instead of major.

17. The terms relative major and relative minor, denote a major key and a minor key which have the same signature.

18. The relative minor key is distinguished from the relative major, by the accidental natural or sharp employed for the leading-note of the minor key.

19. The 6th degree of the major key is the key-note of the relative minor, and the inversion of this—the third degree of the minor key—is the key-note of the relative major; thus, A minor is the relative minor to C (distinguished from it by the accidental G sharp), and C is the relative major to A minor.

SCALE OF C MINOR.

ARBITRARY MINOR SCALE.

20. Certain modifications of the minor scale are sometimes employed in order to avoid the use of the interval of the augmented 2nd in melody (Chap. III. sect. 2).

21. As it is desirable in all scales to rise to the key-note by the step of a semitone, it is allowable, in the ascending minor scale, to make the 6th degree major, and so avoid the step of an augmented 2nd from the 6th to the 7th degree; thus—

22. As it is desirable in the minor scales to fall to the dominant by the step of a semitone, it is allowable, in the descending minor scale, to make the 7th degree minor, and so avoid the step of an augmented 2nd from the 7th to the 6th degree; thus—

23. These arbitrary alterations of the notes of the minor key for the purposes of melody, are available as passing notes (Chap. VII. sects. 4 and 5). The major 6th should never be used as an essential note of a diatonic chord, and the minor 7th is only available as such in one exceptional instance (Chap. IV. sect. 25).

CHROMATIC SCALE.

24. The arrangement with reference to the key-note, of the notes of the major and minor scales, is not more definite than is that of the chromatic scale, though, for convenience of writing, this latter is frequently disregarded, while the former is universally observed; it is necessary, however, to know the notation of the chromatic scale in each key—all the more familiarly on account of its being so often incorrectly written—in order to know the *treatment* of the notes, which being carried out, their nomenclature is of comparatively less importance.

25. The chromatic scale has twelve degrees. These consist of the seven notes of the major key, with the three indicated by the change of signature in the minor key (namely, the minor 3rd, minor 6th, and minor 7th), and the minor 2nd (Chap. IV. sect. 33), and the augmented 4th (Chap. IV. sect. 32). Every interval that can be major or minor is major and minor, and the 4th is the only perfect interval that is changed; this 4th, too, is the only note of the major scale that is raised.

26. The chromatic scale is the same in the major and minor keys.

CHROMATIC SCALE IN THE KEY OF C.

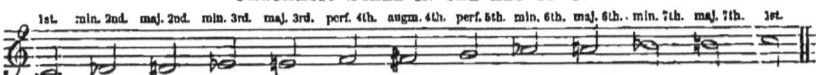

27. Whatever irregularities sometimes occur in the notation of the chromatic scale, composers of all schools agree in writing the augmented 4th from the key-note (not the diminished 5th), and the minor 7th from the key-note (not the augmented 6th).

CHAPTER III.

PROGRESSION OF PARTS.*

1. A PART in harmony is a succession of notes that may be performed by one voice, or by an instrument capable of sounding but one note at a time; as many notes as are sounded together, in so many parts is the harmony.

MELODIC PROGRESSION (Definitions, sect. 1).

2. A part should not proceed by an augmented interval:—

Except; Firstly, in one of the repetitions of a sequence (Chap. VI. sect. 2).
Secondly, in ascending or descending the harmonic minor scale when the top part moves in 6ths with the bass :—

Thirdly, in resolving the fundamental minor 9th (Chap. XI. sect. 22).
Fourthly, in a succession of passing notes framed upon the harmonic minor scale (Chap. VII. sect. 14).
Fifthly, in an arpeggio, or where the two notes belong to the same chord (Definitions, s. 9).

And Sixthly, when the note to which the skip is made is a passing note (Chap. VII. sect. 9).

3. If a part proceed by a diminished interval, it must return to some note within that interval; and not continue in the same

direction ;

HARMONIC PROGRESSION.—CONCORDS (Definitions, sects. 2 and 14).

4. The major and minor concords may be taken in succession between any of the parts 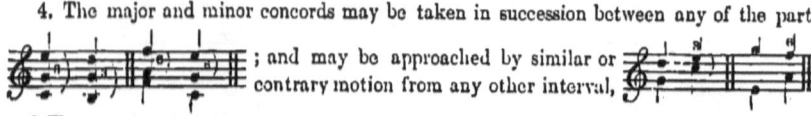 ; and may be approached by similar or contrary motion from any other interval,

* The exceptions in this chapter should not be studied until some advance has been made in the Progressive Exercises.

5. The perfect concords, on the contrary, are subject to many restrictions with regard to their succession, and the manner of approaching them (Chap. I. sect. 9).

6. No two parts may proceed in perfect 5ths with each other,

Yet a 5th may be used in each of two succeeding chords, but it must be assigned to a different part in one chord from that which bears it in the other chord; thus, where, the 5th to the bass is in the middle part in the first chord, and in the top part in the second chord; the extreme (or outside) parts proceed from 3rd to 5th, the top and the middle parts proceed from 6th to 3rd, and the bass and the middle parts proceed from 5th to 3rd, , and so, while both chords contain a 5th, no two parts proceed in 5ths with each other (Chap. III. sect. 26).

7. No two parts may proceed in 8ths or in unisons with each other;

or,

Yet an 8th or an unison may be used in each of two succeeding chords, under the same condition as the 5th: thus, where the 8th of the bass is in the 3rd part from the top in the first chord, and in the top part in the second chord; and thus, where the second and third parts are in unison, in the first chord, and the third and bass parts are in unison in the second chord.

This rule does not apply to the doubling of any one or the whole of the parts throughout a piece, as is the custom in a band, and in a chorus; neither does it apply to the doubling any one part throughout a complete phrase to render it specially prominent, as is frequently done in music for a band or for the pianoforte. The objection is to the progression of *two* parts in 8ths, or in unison. It is always allowable, however, to let the harmony cease, and to make all the parts proceed in 8ths, or in unison, for a complete phrase, or for any portion of a phrase, or to make one part proceed alone without accompaniment (Chap. III. sect. 25).

. *The rules in sections 6 and 7 apply to any two parts, whether extreme parts or middle parts.*

8. The extreme (that is the top and bottom) parts may not proceed by similar motion to a perfect 5th from another interval:—

Except firstly, the 5th of the dominant, if approached from the harmony of the key-note, and the 5th of the key-note, if approached from the harmony of the subdominant; provided

in both cases, the top part move a 2nd,

And except, secondly, any 5th, when changing from one to another position or inversion of the same chord,

9. The extreme parts may not proceed by similar motion to an 8th or an unison, from

any interval,  Except, firstly, the 8th of

the key-note, if approached from the harmony of the dominant, and the 8th of the

subdominant, if approached from the harmony of the key-note, provided in both cases the top part move a 2nd, and provided such 8th be the root of a chord,

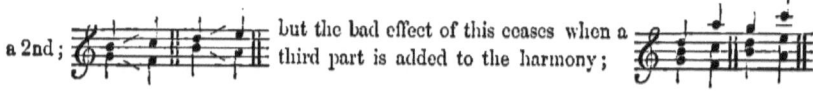

And except, secondly, the 8th of the dominant and the 8th of the key-note, when the top part rises a 2nd, and the bass rises a 4th, and when the top part rises a 4th and the bass rises a 2nd, provided such octave be the 5th from the root of the chord:—

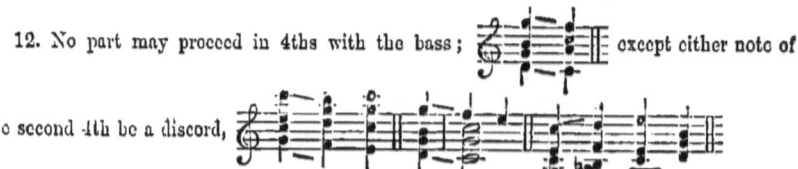

(Definitions, sect. 7).*

10. In harmony of two parts, a 3rd may not be followed by a 5th, when both parts move a 2nd; but the bad effect of this ceases when a third part is added to the harmony;

11. It is not desirable for a lower part to proceed to a higher note in one chord than the note assigned to a higher part in the previous chord; nor for a higher part to proceed to a lower note in one chord, than that assigned to a lower part in the previous chord:

12. No part may proceed in 4ths with the bass; except either note of

the second 4th be a discord,

The progression of 4ths, however, between two upper parts against a moving bass, thus—

 is unobjectionable.

* Appendix B.

13. The leading-note, in a full close (Definitions, sect. 20), **must rise to the key-note—** In any other progression from chord to chord (save when it is a discord, requiring to fall to its resolution), the leading-note must rise; but, save in a full close, there is no restriction as to the interval by which it must rise—

Except, when the bass descends by degrees from the key-note to the 6th of the key, when the leading-note may bear the first inversion of a concord :—

And except in a succession of first inversions (Chap. IV. sect. 16), when all the parts proceed by degrees (Chap. IV. sect. 3).*

₊ *This rule holds in the free style of harmony only ; in the strict or diatonic style, the leading-note is free to rise or to fall.*

14. The leading-note, in changing from one to another position or inversion of the same chord, is free to rise, to fall, or to remain—

As a passing-note (Chap. VII. sect. 3) also, the leading-note is free to rise or to fall.

HARMONIC PROGRESSION.—DISCORDS†(Definitions, sect. 15).

15. No two parts may proceed in 2nds or in 7ths with each other ;

16. No two notes next to each other in alphabetical order may proceed by similar motion to the 8th or unison ;

17. No two notes next to each other in alphabetical order may proceed by oblique motion (that is, where one moves and the other remains) to an 8th, or unison, except in the case of a passing-note (Chap. VII. sect. 1), or of a suspension (Chap. VIII. sect. 3), or of a fundamental 7th in its second inversion (Chap. X. sect. 18), or of a fundamental 9th (Chap. XI. sect. 15).‡

18. The interval of the 9th may not be approached by similar motion :—

19. No two parts should proceed from the interval of an 8th to that of a 7th, when one steps a 2nd and the other leaps a 3rd down.

* Appendix C. † Appendix AA. ‡ Appendix D.

c 2

FALSE RELATION.

20. False relation is when one part has a natural note, and another part has a sharp or flat note of the same name; either when both notes are sounded in the same chord—

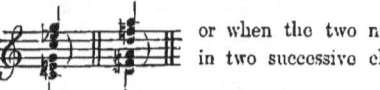 or when the two notes are sounded in two successive chords—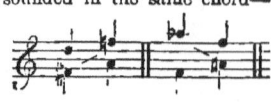

or when the two notes are sounded in two chords with a chord intervening—  In all three forms, false relation is unallowable.

*** *Apparent violations of this rule are to be found in cases of incorrect notation* (Chap. II. sect. 24), *to which, of course, the rule does not apply.*

21. False relation does not exist between two successive chords, when the third of the first chord is the root of the second chord;

and when the 3rd of the first chord is the 5th of the second chord.

22. False relation does not exist between two chords with a chord intervening, when the chromatic note forms part of a fundamental discord (Definitions, sect. 19) ;

when the former of the two chords contains the minor 7th of the arbitrary scale (Chap. IV. sect 25) ;

and also when the first chord is a dominant or a tonic, and the third chord (having its root a minor third below that of the first chord), is the dominant of another key,—but in this case if the intervening chord contain the note which is a 2nd above the root of the third chord, such 2nd must be minor (Chap. XV. sect. 6).*

Pad.

23. Either of the two notes may be doubled (that is, sounded in two parts at once), and the duplicate note in one part stands in no false relation with the note that is chromatically altered in another part :—

24. Chromatic passing notes (Chap. VII. sect. 15) induce no false relation, if all the rules for their treatment be observed.

EXCEPTIONAL PROGRESSION.

25. It is allowable, in the extreme parts, to proceed, by *contrary motion*, from 8th to 8th, between the tonic and dominant,

and between the tonic and subdominant,  (Chap. III. sect. 7.)

* Appendix E.

26. It is allowable, in the extreme parts, to proceed, by *contrary* and by *similar* **motions**

from 5th to 5th, between the tonic and dominant;

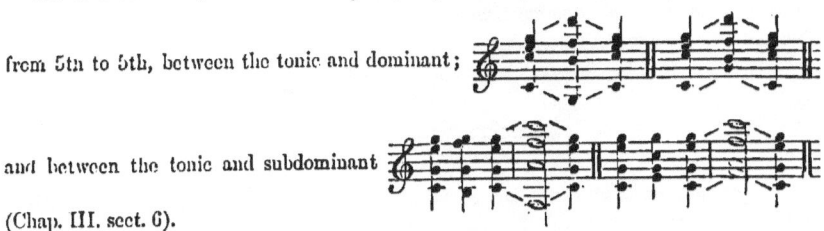

and between the tonic and subdominant

(Chap. III. sect. 6).

*** *The application of these two last rules demands the most careful discretion, and should only be made for the purpose of producing some particular effect.*

CHAPTER IV.
CONCORDS AND THEIR INVERSIONS.

1. A COMMON chord is a bass note (which is the root of the chord, and by which the chord is named), with its perfect 5th and major or minor third; and according as the 3rd is major or minor, it is a major or minor common chord.

2. Either of the notes of a common chord may be doubled; the root, or the 5th, or the 3rd; but it is more frequently desirable to double the root than either of the other two notes.

3. The leading-note, however, may never be doubled, whatever interval in a chord it may form. (Chap. III. sects. 13 and 14; Chap. VI. sect. 3.)

4. The 5th of a common chord may be omitted, and thus the harmony consists of the root and the 3rd only, or of these two, with either or both of them doubled:—

5. The 3rd should not be omitted, except in very rare and peculiar cases.

COMMON CHORDS IN THE MAJOR KEY.

6. There is no common chord on the leading-note, because this note bears a diminished 5th

7. The common chord on the 3rd degree of the major key is questionable as a concord, because of the harsh effect it produces in relation with other chords of the key;

8. There are, then, but five common chords available as concords in the major key; those upon the key-note, the subdominant, and the dominant, are major; those upon the 2nd and 6th, are minor.

9. The common chord of the 2nd of the key may not be followed by the common chord of the key-note :—

Except, firstly, when *both* chords are in the first inversion (Chap. IV. sect. 16),

And except, secondly, when the chord of the key-note is in the second inversion (Chap. IV. sect. 20) :—

Recommendations.

I. Harmony has a richer, fuller effect, when the parts stand at nearly equal distances from one another:—

than when one is at a greater distance from the rest, than those are from one another,

If, however, it be desirable to separate any part from the rest, it is better to have the greater distance between the bass and the part next above it,

than between either of the other parts. This last distribution is even desirable, when the bass part is designed to be particularly prominent.

II. It is generally expedient to let the upper parts proceed by the smallest possible motion; and, when any note is common to two successive chords, to retain it in the same part; thus—

rather than thus,

III. When the bass moves a 2nd it is expedient to make the parts which have the 5th and 8th proceed in contrary motion to the bass :—

Common Chords in the Minor Key.

10. There is no common chord on the leading-note of the minor key, because, as in the major, this note bears a diminished 5th ⸻ (Chap. IV. sect. 6).

11. There is no common chord on the 2nd of the minor key, because this note also bears a diminished 5th ⸻

12. There is no common chord on the 3rd of a minor key, because this note bears an augmented 5th ⸻

13. There are, then, but four common chords in the minor key. those on the key-note and the sub-dominant are minor; those on the dominant and the 6th of the key are major :—

The only common chord that is the same in both the major and the minor keys, is that of the dominant, which is always major.*

A major common chord of the key-note is sometimes used for the full close (Def. sect. 20` in the minor key; the employment of this is more common in ancient than in modern music, and is exceptionally included in the strict or diatonic style (Def. sect. 21). †

First Inversion of Concords in the Major Key.

14. An inversion of a chord is a chord with either of its notes, instead of the root, for the bass.

15. A common chord, having two notes besides the root, has two inversions.

16. The first inversion of a common chord is the chord with its 3rd for the bass, when the root, being placed above the 3rd, becomes the 6th to the bass, and the 5th of the original chord becomes the 3rd to the bass,

17. The interval of the diminished 5th is a discord only when it stands between the bass and an upper part (Chap. IV. sect. 6); it loses its dissonant effect when a bass is placed below it ;

Therefore, though there is no common chord upon the leading-note, the first inversion of a chord (that is, the 3rd and 6th to the bass), may be taken on the 2nd of the key, and treated in every respect as the first inversion of a concord, subject to the same condition as the common chord on the dominant, namely, that the leading-note may not be doubled (Chap. IV. sect. 3).

18. Dissonant as is the effect, in relation with other chords in the key, of the 5th upon the 3rd degree of the major key (Chap. IV. sect. 7.) this is only when it stands between the bass and an upper part, and its dissonance ceases when a bass is placed below it,

Therefore, though the common chord on the 3rd of the major key is un-available as a concord, the first inversion of a chord (that is, the 3rd and 6th to the bass), may be taken on the 5th of the key, and treated in every respect as the first inversion of a concord, under the same condition with regard to the leading-note as the chord last described.

* Appendix BB.　　　† The 3rd in this chord is usually called the " Tierce de Picardie."

19. There is, then, the first inversion of a triad on every note of the major key—

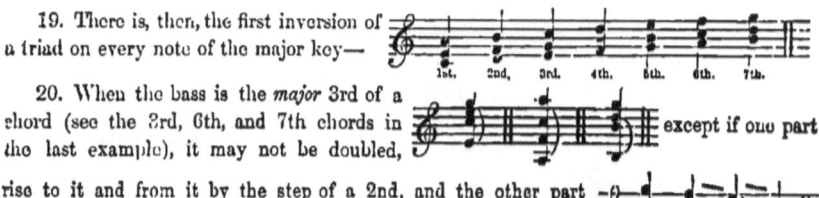

20. When the bass is the *major* 3rd of a chord (see the 3rd, 6th, and 7th chords in the last example), it may not be doubled, except if one part rise to it and from it by the step of a 2nd, and the other part fall to it and from it by the step of a 2nd; thus—

and except if the note be retained or repeated from the previous chord. *

Recommendation.

When several first inversions occur in succession, it is expedient to place the root of each chord (the 6th to the bass) in the top part, and the 5th of each chord (the 3rd to the bass) in an under part;

rather than to have the inversion of this position, which would induce a succession of 5ths;

First Inversion of Concords in the Minor Key.

21. In the minor key, as in the major, the triad on the leading-note, though dissonant in its original position (Chap IV. sect. 10) is available in its first inversion as the first inversion of a concord (Chap. IV. sect. 17).

22. Upon the same principle (Chap. IV. sect. 17), the triad on the 2nd of the minor key, though dissonant in its original position (Chap. IV. sect. 11), is available in its first inversion, and treated as the first inversion of a concord—

23. The interval of the augmented 5th is equally dissonant in whatever position it may stand; the triad on the 3rd of the minor key (Chap. IV. sect. 12) can, therefore, not be taken as a concord in any form or inversion. Thus, the 5th of the minor key may not be taken as the bass of a first inversion; it may, however, bear the single interval of the 6th when either the bass or the 6th, or both of these, may be doubled :—

24. There is, then, the first inversion of a triad on every note of the minor key except the 5th, and this note bears the single interval of the 6th—

25. When the bass descends by degrees from the key-note to the 6th of the key, the minor 7th from the key-note may be taken as the bass of a first inversion—

(Chap. II. sect. 23: Chap. III. sect. 22).

* Appendix EE.

SECOND INVERSION OF COMMON CHORDS.

26. The second inversion of a common chord is the chord with its 5th in the bass, when the root becomes the 4th to the bass, and the 3rd of the original chord becomes the 6th to the bass

27. In both the major and the minor key the only common chords that can be taken in the second inversion, are those of the key-note, the subdominant, and the dominant. The dominant (being the 5th of the key-note), the key-note (being the 5th of the subdominant), and the supertonic (being the 5th of the dominant), are the three bass-notes of these second inversions—

28. The bass may not approach a second inversion by leap from the inversion of another chord; * but may, by step of a 2nd from the inversion of another chord, it may, by leap from an inversion of the same chord, and it may, by leap or by step of a 2nd from the root of another or the same chord :—

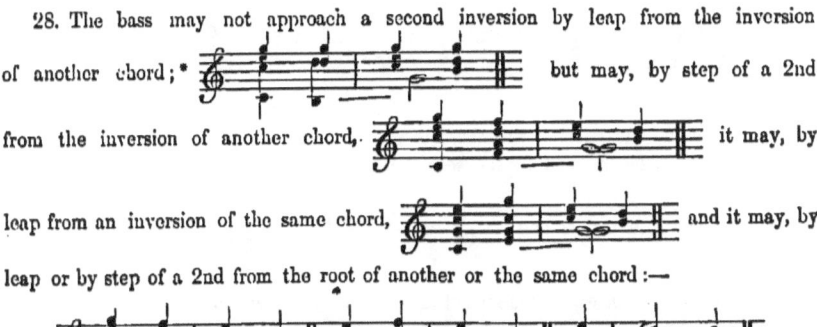

29. A second inversion must be followed either by some other chord upon the same bass note (or its octave); or else by some chord on the note next above or below it, diatonic or chromatic :—

So long as the same harmony continues, the bass of a second inversion may proceed to another note of the chord, or may have any succession of passing notes; provided when the harmony changes to a chord having another root, the bass return to the note that has the second inversion, or to the note next above or below it, whichever it might have taken had t made no such digression :—

---

* Except from the third inversion of a chord containing a fundamental 7th (Chap. X. sect. 25), and from the second inversion of a chord containing an 11th (Chap. XII. sect. 20).

D

30. A second inversion, if followed by a chord on the *same* bass-note, must be at a more strongly accented part of the bar, than the chord which follows it :—

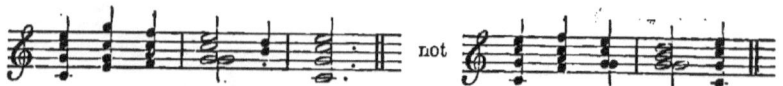

Except only, if the second inversion have been preceded by another chord on the same bass-note, when it may be taken at any part of the bar :—

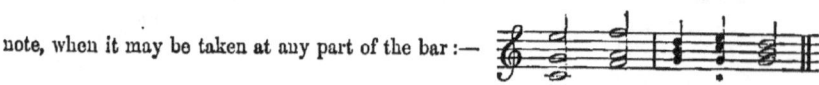

A second inversion, if followed by a chord upon the next note, may be either at the stronger or weaker part of the bar :—

31. The second inversion of the chord of the dominant (having the 2nd of the key for its bass-note) may be followed by the second inversion of the chord of the subdominant (having the key-note for its bass), 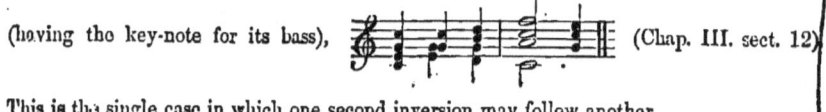 (Chap. III. sect. 12)

This is the single case in which one second inversion may follow another.

CHROMATIC CONCORDS. (Defin. sect. 12.)

In the Minor Key.

32. A major common chord may be taken on the supertonic of the minor key, of which the 3rd and 5th are chromatic notes—†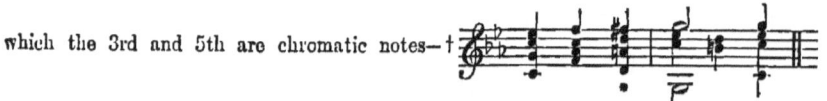

The 3rd of this chromatic chord (being the augmented 4th of the key-note), may *never* be doubled, and in proceeding to another chord, this note must either rise or fall a semitone. In order not to induce a modulation into the key of the dominant, this chromatic chord must be followed either by a chord containing the diatonic 4th of the key—

or else by some form of the common chord of the key-note :—*

* Appendix F.   † Appendix U

The first inversion of the chromatic chord of the supertonic (having the augmented 4th of the key-note for its bass), may be taken under the same condition, as the chord in its original position :— *

33. A major common chord may be taken on the minor 2nd of the minor key, of which the root is a chromatic note :—

There is no restriction as to what chord in the key must follow this chromatic chord.

The first inversion of this chromatic chord of the minor 2nd of the key may also be taken. The bass-note of this inversion, though the major 3rd to the root, may be doubled at discretion :—

The chord in this inversion is sometimes called the chord of the "Neapolitan 6th."†

In the Major Key.

34. All the concords peculiar to the minor key,—except the minor chord of the key-note and its two inversions,—may be taken as chromatic chords in the major key.

35. There are then, besides the diatonic concords (Chap. IV. sects. 8, 19, 27), the following chromatic concords in the major key :—

I. A minor common chord on the subdominant, and its first and second inversions:—

II. The first inversion on the subdominant of a triad with a diminished 5th (Chap. IV. sect. 22) :—

III. A major common chord on the minor 6th of the key and its first inversion : —

IV. A major common chord on the supertonic and its first inversion, subject to the same conditions as in the minor key (Chap. IV. sect. 32):—

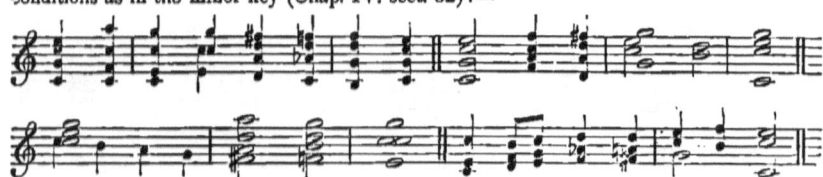

V. A major common chord on the minor 2nd of the key and its first inversion (Chap. IV. sect. 33):—

CHAPTER V.

PEDALS.

1. A PEDAL is a bass note sustained through a succession of chords, of which chords the pedal note may or may not form an essential portion.

2. The key-note and the dominant are the only notes that may be employed as pedals: either or both of these may be sustained throughout any passage, diatonic or chromatic, that does not modulate. Were the key changed, the pedal note would no longer be the key-note or the dominant.* The following examples of pedals, each of which is in one key throughout, are correct—

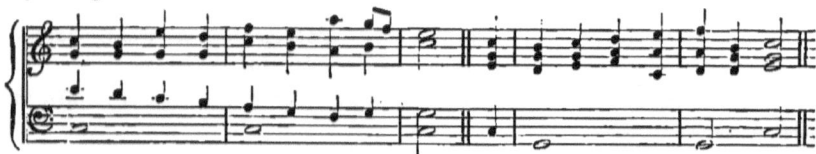

but the following examples, in which modulations occur, are unallowable (Chap. V. sects. 7 and 8)—

3. When the pedal-note is not an essential portion of the harmony, the part next above it should form a good bass (that is, should not have any notes unallowable as bass-notes, or proceed by leaps that are unallowable in the bass). When the pedal-note is an essential portion of the harmony, the part next above it, if the 5th of a chord, is not to be regarded as bearing a second inversion. The following example is faulty on account of the con-

* Appendix Q

secutive 4ths at 4, 4 (Chap. III. sect. 12); and on account of the leap from C, which is to be regarded as bearing a second inversion at * (Chap. IV. sect. 29).

4. A pedal mostly commences with the harmony of which the pedal-note is the root; as in the foregoing examples. It may, however, commence with any harmony of which the pedal-note is or is not an essential portion.

5. A pedal-note can only be quitted when it is an essential portion of the harmony; if this be the 5th of a chord or a discord requiring resolution, the rules for its treatment must be observed as though there had been no pedal. The following example is faulty, because the C pedal is quitted upon the chord of G, of which C is not an essential portion—

The following examples are correct, because the pedal notes are quitted upon chords of which they are essential portions—

6. A pedal may close with a modulation, provided no change of key take place until the last chord upon the pedal (Chap. V. sect. 2) :—

7. The last inversion of the chromatic chord of the minor 13th (Chap. XIII. sect. 12), and its resolution upon the same bass, are not to be regarded as forming a pedal. This harmony may be employed to make a modulation at the close of a pedal.

8. One only series of harmonies foreign to the key, the employment of which involve a transient modulation, is allowable upon a pedal. This is the major common chord of the sixth degree of the major key, and the fundamental discords derived from the same root, any of which may be used upon a dominant pedal, provided it be followed by some chord of which the perfect 4th of the key-note (the 7th of the dominant) is a portion :—

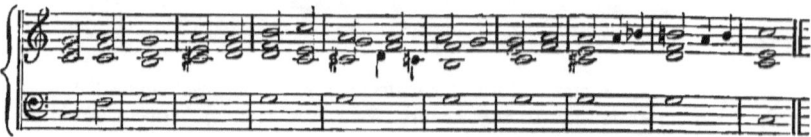

This is a single exception from the rule in sect. 2.

9. Any note may be sustained throughout a succession of passing-notes in one, in two, or more parts (Chap. VII. sect. 7) :—

Instances of this must not be mistaken for pedals, against which the harmony may proceed independently of the pedal note, making any progressions that might be employed without the pedal.

INVERTED PEDALS.

10. In modern music the pedal is frequently inverted, that is, an upper part sustains a note throughout a succession of chords, of which chords the pedal note may or may not form an essential portion; thus—

11. All the rules for the bass pedal apply to the inverted pedal, except only the rule in sect. 3; the inverted pedal in no way affects the progression of the bass part, so long as this remains in the key of which the pedal note is the tonic or the dominant.

12. Sometimes the bass pedal is doubled in an upper part, in which case all the rules for its treatment apply without exception.

CHAPTER VL

SEQUENCES.

1. A SEQUENCE is the repetition of a progression of harmony, upon other notes of the scale, when all the parts proceed by the same degrees in each repetition as in the original progression; thus, in the following progression, the bass rises a 4th, the top part falls a 2nd, the part next to the top rises a 2nd, and the part next to the bass falls a 3rd—

 and in this repetition of the same progression, each part moves by the same number of degrees—

2. In a sequence the name of the interval in the original progression (as 2nd, 3rd, 4th, &c.) and not its quality (as major or minor, perfect or augmented) is preserved in the repetitions. Thus, in a sequence of melody an augmented interval may be employed in one of the repetitions of what was a perfect interval in the original progression, as at *

without the harsh effect this interval would produce apart from the sequence (Chap. III. sect. 2). In like manner in a sequence of harmony, the dissonant 5ths on the 3rd and 7th of the major key, and on the 2nd, 3rd, and 7th of the minor key, may be employed in the repetitions of what were consonant 5ths in the original progression as at *

In the last example it may be observed that the top part moves a major 2nd in the original progression, and in the first, the second, and the fourth repetition, but a minor 2nd in the third repetition; the part next to the top moves a minor 2nd in the original progression, and in the fourth repetition, but a major 2nd in the first, the second, and the third repetitions; the part next to the bass moves a minor 3rd in the original progression, and in the first, the third, and the fourth repetitions, but a major 3rd in the second repetition; and the bass moves a perfect 4th in all cases but the third repetition, where it moves an augmented 4th.

3. Upon the same principle the leading-note may be doubled in one of the repetitions of a sequence, as in the fourth bar of the last example (Chap. IV. sect. 3).

4. The original progression in a sequence may consist of two chords, as in the foregoing examples; or of more than two chords, as in the examples that are to come. It

may consist of concords only; or of these intermixed with passing notes; or with prepared discords —

The 2nd inversion of concords is unavailable in sequences.

5. The repetitions of a sequence may be upon successively higher degrees of the scale, as in the foregoing examples; or upon successively lower degrees, thus :—

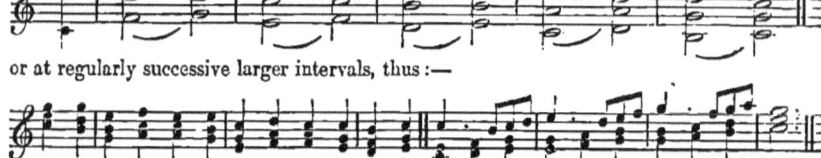

or at regularly successive larger intervals, thus :—

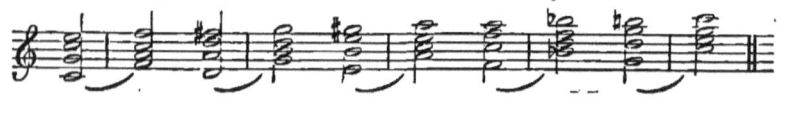

6. When a progression is repeated in a different key, none of the rules for sequences justifying the exceptional treatment of particular notes apply; thus, in the following example, where every accidental sharp, flat, and natural induces a modulation, each progression is entirely independent of the others, and each is satisfactory in itself—

CHAPTER VII.

PASSING NOTES.

1. PASSING-NOTES are notes which do not belong to chords, and are therefore inessential to the harmony. They are employed in one or more parts, and resolve either upon a note of the chord against which they are taken;

or else upon a note of another chord; A passing-note may proceed by oblique motion to an 8th ;  but *should* not proceed to

an unison ; (Chap. III. sect. 17.)

IN THE STRICT OR DIATONIC STYLE.

2. A passing-note must be approached and quitted by the step of a 2nd—and it must be at a less accented part of the bar than the harmony-note which precedes it.

3. A passing-note approached in this manner may either rise or fall to the

next note ;  If the note to which it passes be

also inessential to the harmony, this second passing-note may not return to the first, but must proceed up or down in the direction in which it was approached ;

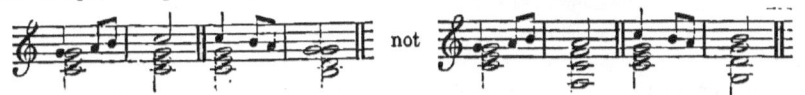 not

and the passage must continue in this direction until it reaches a harmony-note.

4. The major 6th from the key-note of the arbitrary minor scale (Chap. II. sect. 21) may be employed as a passing-note ascending or descending, when the 5th and major 7th of the key are harmony-notes :—

Also in a passage ascending from the 5th of the key to the key-note in which these two are harmony-notes, the major 6th of the  arbitrary minor scale may be employed as a passing-note :—*

5. The minor 7th from the key-note of the arbitrary minor scale (Chap. II. sect. 22) may be employed as a passing-note, ascending or descending, when the minor 6th of the key and the key-note are harmony-notes :—

Also in a passage descending from the key-note to the 5th of the key in which these two are harmony-notes the minor 7th  of the arbitrary minor scale may be employed as a passing-note :—*

6. A single exception from the rule in sect. 2 is, that a passing-note, instead of proceeding to the harmony-note next to it, may skip a 3rd to the note on the other side of such

harmony-note, when this note to which the skip is made must return to the harmony-note between the two :—

7. If more than one part at a time proceed by passing-notes, the parts which move while other parts sustain must proceed in such progressions with each other as would make pure harmony, independently of the sustaining parts :—

At those places, however, where the chords change and all the parts move together, the motion of the accompanying parts fills up any incompleteness in the harmony of those parts which proceed by passing notes; the 4th between the two top parts at the beginning of the second bar in the next example is unobjectionable, because, the lower parts move when the upper parts come upon this interval, but the 4th which follows it is faulty, because, as only the two top parts move, the lower of these two must be regarded as a bass to the

upper (Chap. III. sect. 12).

8. Two parts may proceed by the step of a 2nd in contrary motion from a concord to a discord, and this discord may either be resolved by the return of both parts to the concord

from which they proceeded—  or else in both parts it may proceed by

the step of a 2nd in contrary motion, when if the note thus approached be also a discord, both parts must continue to proceed in contrary motion until they reach a harmony-note; thus—

Either or both of the parts so proceeding in contrary motion, may be accompanied by another part proceeding in 3rds or 6ths with it,

or one part may proceed in one direction, ascending or descending, while three other parts proceed in the contrary direction in the relation of 1st, 3rd, and 6th to each other :—

In the Free, or Chromatic Style.

9. A passing-note may be approached by the step of a 2nd, as in the strict style. It may also be approached by leap, and, in this case, even by an augmented interval :—

 (Chap. III. sect. 2). It must always be quitted by the step of a 2nd; and it may be at either a more or less accented part of the bar.

10. If a passing-note that is approached by leap resolve upon the harmony note below it, the passing-note may be at the interval of a tone or a semitone from its resolution, according to the diatonic scale :—

11. If a passing-note approached by leap resolve on the harmony-note above it, the passing-note must, when it resolves on the root, the 5th, or the 7th of a chord, be at the interval of a semitone from its resolution :—

 not

When it resolves on the 3rd of a chord it may be at the interval of a tone or a semitone,

In case of the exceptional leap of a 3rd from a passing-note to the note beyond the harmony-note on which it is resolved (Chap. VII. sect. 6), if this harmony-note be the root, the 5th, or the 7th of a chord, the passing-note below it must be at the interval of a semitone,

12. A passing-note approached by the step of a descending 2nd from the root or the 5th of the chord, and returning upwards to the same note, must be at the interval of a semitone from its resolution :—*

* Appendix I.

13. If in a succession of passing-notes, a chromatic note be taken, the passage must proceed by semitones till it reaches a harmony-note, thus:—

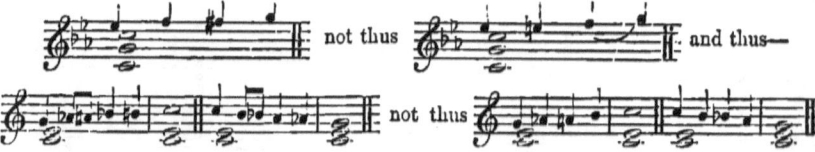

In the following example, the chromatic passing-note, A flat, proceeds by a semitone to A natural, which is a fundamental major 9th to the root, and this is resolved upon the 3rd (Chap. XI. sect. 31); as, therefore, the A natural is a harmony-note, here is no exception from the rule:—

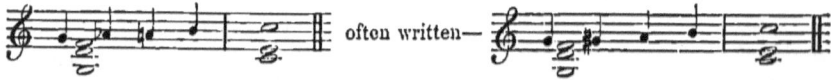

In the following example, when the key is minor (since the major 9th of the dominant is in this case unallowable; Chap. XI. sect. 29); the A natural is a chromatic passing-note, and, therefore, the passage should proceed by semitones from it, till it reaches B natural, the next harmony-note:—

14. The harmonic minor scale (Chap. II. sect. 15) may be employed for a succession of passing notes upon the dominant harmony in the minor key, when the interval of the augmented 2nd (between the 6th and 7th degrees) is unobjectionable (Chap. III. sect. 2):—

It is also employed, but less frequently, for a succession of passing-notes upon other harmonics, in the minor key:—

The major 6th and minor 7th of the arbitrary minor scale are also available for passing-notes, as in the strict style (Chap. VII. sects. 4 and 5).

15. The note a semitone below any interval of a chord may be taken by leap as a passing-note, if it be resolved upwards, without producing false relation with the harmony-note on which it resolves:—

A note a semitone above any interval may be taken by descent of a semitone, if it be resolved downwards, without producing false relation with the harmony-note on which it resolves :—

CHAPTER VIII.

SUSPENSIONS.

1. SUSPENSION is the retaining of a note of one chord, while another chord is sounded, of which this note forms no portion. Such note must be retained or suspended in the part to which it is assigned in the first chord, not newly sounded in a different part; and it must proceed to a note of the chord over which it is suspended :—*

The sounding of the note in the first chord is the preparation of the discord; the suspension is the discord, and its progression to a note of the second chord is the resolution of the discord.

It must be understood, that to suspend, retain, or hold on a note from one chord, instead of proceeding directly to a note of another chord, is equivalent to one part moving behind the time of the rest, and that no note newly sounded in any part is a suspended note. The D in the following example is therefore no suspension, since it is not held on in the part next to the bass, in which the D of the first chord should prepare it; but newly sounded in the top part without preparation :—

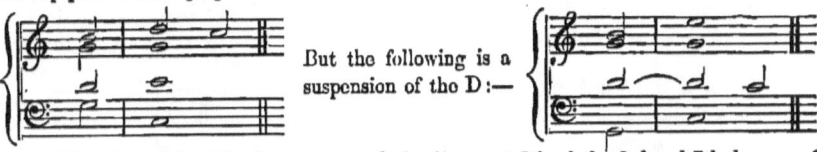

But the following is a suspension of the D :—

2. The 9th and the 4th of any root, and the dissonant 5th of the 3rd and 7th degrees of the major and the minor key are the only intervals that may be suspended.

* Appendix J.

3. A suspended discord may not be sounded together with the note upon which it is resolved, except the 9th. together with the root in the bass:—

And except the 9th together with the root in an upper part, when the root must be approached by step of a 2nd; and except the 4th, together with the 3rd in either the bass or an upper part, when the 3rd must be approached by step of a 2nd:—

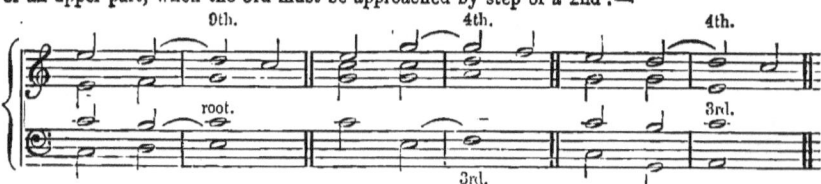

These last exceptions, though admissible, are undesirable, and should only be employed with the most careful discretion. In all the exceptional cases the root and the 3rd must be at the interval of an 8th from the resolution of the discord. The suspended 5th on the 3rd and 7th of the key can never be sounded together with the note on which it is resolved.

4. A suspended discord always stands instead of the note upon which it is resolved; and where this note may not be taken, the suspended discord that must be resolved upon it may not be taken; thus, since the following progressions of concords are unallowable,

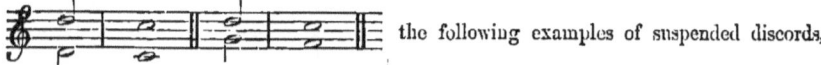 the following examples of suspended discords,

which are resolved upon such unallowable concords, are equally unallowable:— *

5. A suspension is accompanied exactly as the note upon which it is resolved would be if there were no suspension, subject only to the conditions stated in sect. 3; thus, the chord is always known by the resolution, the suspended note being inessential to the harmony.†

6. The suspended 9th is resolved upon the root of a chord. It is accompanied by the root in the bass, the 3rd, and the 5th:—

7. The first inversion of the suspended 9th has the 3rd in the bass. As in the first inversion of a common chord the root becomes the 6th to the bass note; so, in the first inversion of a suspended 9th, the 9th (which is a 2nd above the root) becomes the 7th to the bass-note, and is resolved upon the 6th:—

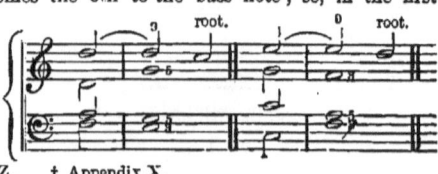

* Appendix Z.   † Appendix X.

Though there is no suspended 9th over those degrees of the major and the minor key that bear not common chords, the first inversion of a suspended 9th may be taken over the first inversion of either of those dissonant triads (Chap. IV. sect. 17, 18, 21, 22):—

8. The second inversion of the suspended 9th has the 5th in the bass, and may only be taken in those three instances in which the second inversion of a common chord is allowable (Chap. IV. sect. 27). As in the second inversion of a common chord, the root becomes the 4th to the bass; so, in the second inversion of a suspended 9th, the 9th (which is a 2nd above the root) becomes the 5th to the bass-note, and is resolved upon the 4th:—

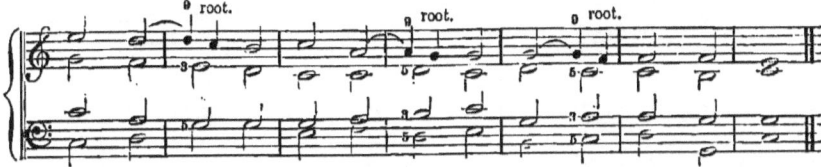

9. The last inversion of the suspended 9th has the 9th in the bass. As the 9th is a 2nd above the root, the 3rd of the original chord now becomes the 2nd to the bass, and the 5th of the original chord now becomes the 4th to the bass; the root may be taken above the 9th if approached by the step of a 2nd (Chap. VIII. sect. 3), but it is preferable to double either of the other notes rather than to take this. The 7th, 4th, and 2nd being continued while the bass is resolved, they become the 8th, 5th, and 3rd to the resolution:—

10. The suspended 4th is resolved on the 3rd:—

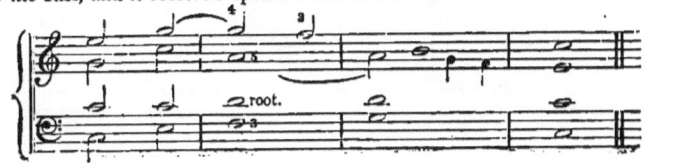

11. The first inversion of a suspended 4th has the 3rd in the bass, which must be approached by the step of a 2nd under the condition stated in sect. 3. The 4th now becomes the 9th to the bass, and is resolved upon the 8th to the bass:—

Though there is no suspended 4th over those degrees of the major and the minor keys that bear not common chords, the first inversion of a suspended 4th may be taken over the first inversion of either of those dissonant triads (Chap. IV. sects. 17, 18, 21, 22).—

12. The second inversion of the suspended 4th has the 5th in the bass, and may only be taken in those three instances in which the 2nd inversion of a common chord is allowable (Chap. IV. sect. 27). As in the second inversion of a common chord, the 3rd becomes the 6th to the bass, so in the second inversion of a suspended 4th, the 4th (which is the 2nd above the 3rd) becomes the 7th to the bass and is resolved upon the 6th—

13. The last inversion of the suspended 4th has the 4th in the bass, which is resolved upon the 3rd of the original chord, and this, being in the bass, bears a first inversion. The 3rd and 6th to the bass, in the first inversion of a concord, now become the 2nd and 5th; these being retained while the bass is resolved, they then form the first inversion of a concord :—

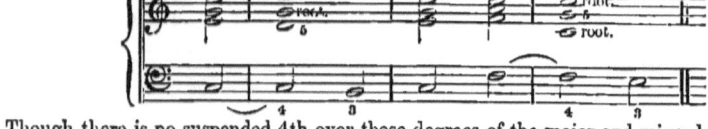

Though there is no suspended 4th over those degrees of the major and minor keys that bear not common chords, the last inversion of a suspended 4th may be taken, which will resolve upon the first inversion of either of those dissonant triads (Chap. IV. sects. 17, 18, 21, 22) :—

14. The dissonant 5th on the 3rd and 7th of the key is resolved upon the 6th of the same bass-note; this 6th being the root of the original chord, the 5th is virtually the 7th; it can, however, never be taken as a 7th, but only in this form of a 5th, so that its resolution produces the first inversion of a common chord :—

On any other bass-note besides these two, the 5th is a concord, and is free to proceed to the 6th or any other note; on the 3rd and 7th of the key, this interval, as a suspended discord, *must* be resolved upón the 6th :—*

15. Any suspension may, previous to its resolution, leap or proceed by step of a 2nd to a consonant note of the same chord, but must return to its resolution before the harmony changes : —

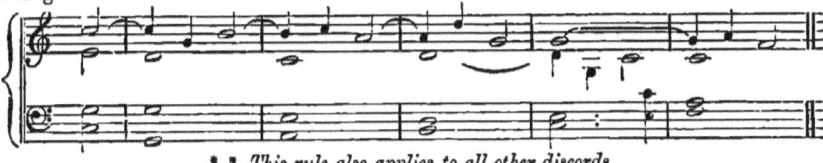

₊ *This rule also applies to all other discords.*

DOUBLE SUSPENSIONS.

16. The 9th and 4th may be suspended together, in the original position of a chord, or in any of its inversions. The rules for their treatment are then precisely the same as when either of them is taken separately :—

17. The dissonant 5th on the 3rd and 7th of the key may be accompanied with the first inversion of a suspended 9th, which resolves upon the 6th to the bass, when the dissonant 5th rises to the same note :—

A dissonant 5th on the 3rd of the key may be accompanied also with the first inversion of a suspended 4th, which is resolved together with the inverted 9th and the dissonant 5th :—

* Appendix CC.   r

SUSPENSION OF COMPLETE CHORDS.

18. When the progression of roots is by the rise of a 4th (as C to F, D to G, &c.), the whole of the first chord may be suspended over the bass of the second, whether this bass be the root or the 3rd of the chord. In this case—there being suspended sufficient notes to define the chord that prepares them,—the notes are regarded not with reference to the bass over which they are suspended, but to the chord that prepares them, and they proceed just as they would were there no suspension, provided only that no dissonant note move more than a 2nd:—

    ⁎ *This rule applies not only to concords, but to all the discords hereafter described.*

19. A fundamental discord (Definitions, sect. 19) may be prepared in one position, and suspended in another:—

or any notes, derived from the same root, may be introduced in the suspension which were not in the chord that prepared it; thus:—

CHAPTER IX.

CHORDS OF THE DISSONANT FIFTH.

1. PASSING-NOTES and suspensions form no portion of chords, and thus are inessential to the harmony. The discords hereafter described form constituent portions of chords, and are thus essential to the harmony.

2. Every diatonic discord of this class is resolved upon a chord, the root of which is a 4th above the root of the discord.

3. The dissonant 5th on the 3rd degree of the minor and the major key (besides being taken as a suspension, which is resolved while the rest of the chord continues) (Chap. VIII.

sect. 14). may be taken as an essential discord, which is resolved when the entire chord changes :—

4. The chord of the augmented 5th on the 3rd degree of the minor key is resolved upon the chord of the submediant. The 5th is the discord which, in whatever position it appears, must be prepared, and must be resolved upon the 3rd of the following chord. This is accompanied with the root and the 3rd, either of which may be doubled, but it is preferable to double the 3rd rather than the root (Chap. X. sect. 7) :—

5. The first inversion of this chord has the 3rd in the bass; the root then becomes the 6th to the bass, and the augmented 5th (the dissonant note) is the 3rd to the bass, and must rise to the 3rd of the next chord :—

6. The triad on the 3rd of the major key is resolved upon the chord of the submediant. The perfect 5th is a discord which must be prepared, and must be resolved upon the 3rd of the following chord. This is accompanied with the root and the 3rd, either of which may be doubled, but it is preferable to double the 3rd rather than the root :—

This chord is dissonant only when it has the root in the bass. In its first inversion it is available as a concord (Chap. IV. sect. 18).

7. The diminished 5th on the 2nd degree of the minor key may be taken as an essential discord, but this may never be used unless accompanied with the 7th (Chap. X. sect. 9).

CHAPTER X.

CHORDS OF THE SEVENTH.

1. A chord of the 7th consists of a triad with a 7th added to it:—

2. A diatonic chord of the 7th must be resolved upon a chord, the root of which is a 4th above the root of the discord, and this second chord may be a concord or another prepared discord:—

(Chap. IX. sect. 2). The first inversion of a chord of the 9th (Chap. XI. sect. 6) presents an apparent but not a real exception from this rule.

3. The 7th is the dissonant-note, which, in whatever position it may be, must be prepared, and must be resolved upon the 3rd of the following chord. Its resolution may be delayed by its being suspended as a 4th (Chap. VIII. sect. 10).

4. A chord of the 7th, having three notes besides the root, has three inversions; the second inversion, however, is unavailable.

5. The first inversion of the chord of the 7th has the 3rd in the bass. The root is then the 6th to the bass, the 7th is the 5th to the bass (requiring the same resolution as in its original position), and the 5th is the 3rd to the bass:—

6. The last inversion of the chord of the 7th has the 7th in the bass, and it must be resolved upon a first inversion of a chord on the note below. The root is then the 2nd to the bass, the 3rd is the 4th to the bass, and the 5th is the 6th to the bass:—

7. A 7th may be added to the chord of the augmented 5th on the mediant of the minor key (Chap. IX. sect. 4), when both the 7th and the 5th have the same treatment as either would have without the other:—

8. A 7th may be added to the triad on the mediant of the major key (Chap. IX. sect. 6), when both the 7th and the 5th have the same treatment as either would have without the other :—

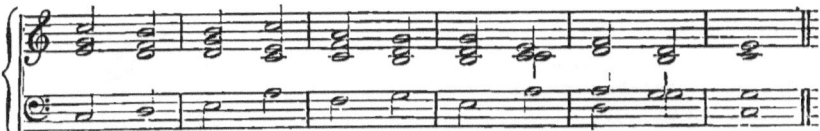

In the inversions of this chord, the 5th is not a discord, and the 7th only has to be prepared and resolved :—

9. A chord of the 7th may be taken on the second degree of the minor key, in which the 5th as well as 7th is a discord (Chap. IX. sect. 7). The 7th has the same treatment as in every other instance; the 5th must be prepared and must be resolved upon the root of the following chord :—

In the inversions of this chord the 5th is not a discord, and the 7th only has to be prepared and resolved :—

10. As there is no common chord upon the leading-note, there can be no chord of the 7th upon the subdominant (Chap. X. sect. 2), except in one of the repetitions of a sequence (Chap. VI. sects. 2 and 3). As, however, the first inversion on the 2nd of the key is available as a concord (Chap. IV. sects. 17, 21), the last inversion of a chord of the 7th of the subdominant may be taken and resolved upon such first inversion :—

11. As there is no common chord upon the 3rd of the major key, there can be no chord of the 7th on the leading-note (Chap. X. sect. 2), except in one of the repetitions of a sequence (Chap. VI. sects. 2, 3). As, however, the first inversion on the 5th of the major key is available as a concord (Chap. IV. sect. 18), the last inversion of a chord of the 7th on the leading-note may be taken and resolved upon such first inversion :—*

THE DOMINANT 7TH.†

12. A chord of the 7th on the dominant may be taken without preparation; but it is resolved, like prepared chords of the 7th, on a chord of which the root is a 4th above the root of the discord,—that is, on the chord of the key-note. The first inversion of the chord

* Appendix K　　　　† Appendix L.

of the 9th of the mediant consists of the same notes as the chord of the 7th of the dominant and its different resolution is regarded by some as an exceptional treatment of the dominant harmony (Chap. XI. sect. 11).*

13. This chord consists of the root, the major 3rd, the perfect 5th, and the minor 7th, which intervals distinguish it from every other chord of the 7th, formed of the notes of the diatonic scale :—

14. In this chord, the 3rd (which is the leading-note), as well as the 7th, requires to be resolved. The root and the 5th, which form a perfect interval with each other (Chap. I. sect. 9), are free in their motion, provided they break none of the rules for the progression of parts.

15. The 3rd, in the chord of the dominant 7th, must rise a 2nd to its resolution, while the 7th falls a 2nd :—

16. Unlike all other diatonic chords of the 7th, that of the dominant may be taken in the second inversion, when the 5th of the original chord is the bass-note, the 3rd is the 6th to the bass, the root is the 4th to the bass, and the 7th is the 3rd to the bass :—

17. The bass, in this case, is restricted in its progression as in the second inversion of a concord (Chap. IV. sect. 29) ; thus, it may fall a 2nd or rise a 2nd :—

18. When the bass of a second inversion of a chord of the 7th rises one degree to the 3rd of the following chord, the 7th may also rise one degree to the 5th of the following chord :—

This treatment of the interval of the 7th forms a single exception from the rules previously given for the resolution of discords (Chap. III. sect. 17 ; Chap. X. sect. 15).

19. In the second inversion of the chord of the dominant 7th, the root may be omitted, and then, but then only, the 7th may be doubled ; in this case, while one 7th falls to the 3rd of the next chord, the other may rise to the 5th, or may even leap upwards to the root of the following chord :—

The notes of this chord are identical with those of a first inversion on the 2nd of the key (Chap. IV. sect. 10, 21), and it is always discretionary to treat it as such, when its progression is free ; or as an inversion of the dominant 7th, when it is resolved upon the chord of the key-note :—   * Appendix M.

20. When the 7th is in the bass, it may not be approached by leap downwards,

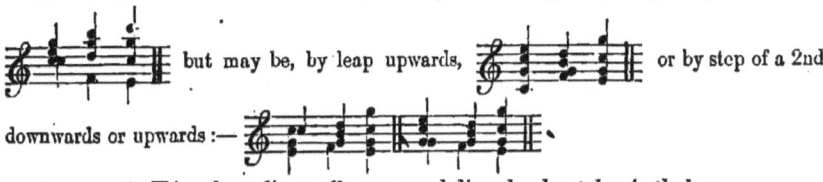

but may be, by leap upwards, or by step of a 2nd downwards or upwards :—

⁎ *This rule applies to all unprepared discords when taken in the bass.*

THE SUPERTONIC 7TH.

21. A chromatic chord of the 7th on the Supertonic may be taken without preparation.

22. This chord consists of the chromatic common chord on the supertonic (Chap. IV. sect. 32), with the addition of the 7th; and its intervals are thus the same as those of the chord of the dominant 7th :—

23. The progression of this chord and the treatment of the 3rd are bound by the rule for the chromatic common chord on the same note (Chap. IV. sect. 32).

24. The 7th in this chord must either fall a 2nd (as in other chords of the 7th), or remain to be a note of the following chord :—

25. When the 7th remains to be a note of the following chord, it may be doubled; and then one of the two 7ths is free to leap as a concord :—

It is also allowable, without doubling the 7th, to make it leap as a concord, provided the 5th in the chord of the 7th proceed to that note in the following chord which was the 7th in this :—*

* Appendix DD.

26. In the second inversion of this chord the root may be omitted, and then the 7th may be doubled, as in the second inversion of the dominant 7th (Chap. X. sect. 19) :—

27. When this chord is followed by the dominant 7th (its 3rd falling a chromatic semitone to the 7th of the following chord), it is allowable for the 7th to rise one degree to the 5th of the following chord, provided the 5th in the first chord proceed to the 3rd in the second chord ; this, however, must be regarded as an exceptional progression, and should therefore be but rarely employed :—

THE TONIC 7TH.

28. A chromatic chord of the 7th on the Tonic may be taken without preparation, in either the major or minor key.

29. This chord consists of the major common chord of the key-note (in which in the minor key the 3rd is chromatic), with the addition of a minor 7th (which in the major key is chromatic), and its intervals are thus the same as those of the chord of the dominant 7th :—

30. In order not to induce a modulation into the key of the subdominant, this chord must be followed either by a dominant discord, or by a supertonic discord :—*

31. The 3rd in this chord may never be doubled. It must either rise a minor second :—

or rise a major 2nd :—   or fall a chromatic semitone :—

32. The 7th in this chord must either rise a chromatic semitone :—

or fall a 2nd :—

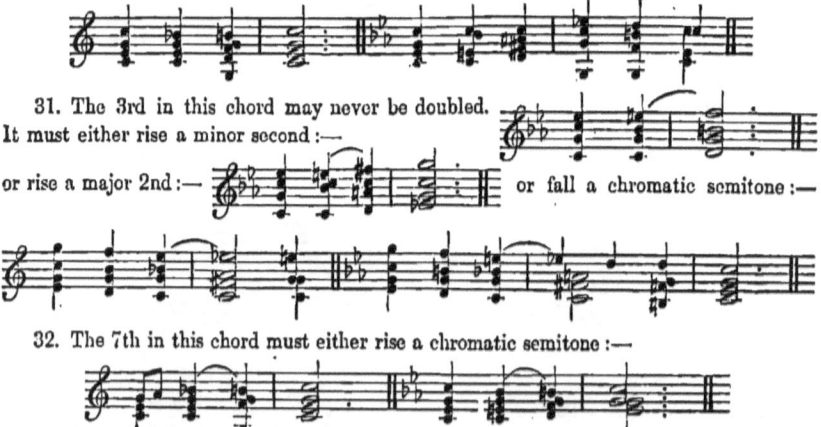

* Appendix N.

33. In the second inversion of this chord the root may be omitted (as in the dominant 7th, Chap. X. sect. 19), but the 7th may not here be doubled :—

34. When this chord is followed by the dominant 7th (its 7th rising a chromatic semi-tone to the 3rd of the following chord), it is allowable for the 3rd to fall one degree to the 5th of the following chord, provided the 5th in the first chord proceed to the 7th in the second chord; this, however, must be regarded as an exceptional progression, and should therefore be but rarely employed :—

CHAPTER XI.

CHORDS OF THE NINTH.

1. A chord of the 9th consists of a chord of the 7th with a 9th added to it :—

2. A diatonic chord of the 9th must be resolved on a concord or discord, the root of which is a 4th above the root of the first chord (Chap. X. sect. 2) :—

3. The 9th is a dissonant note, which, in whatever position it may be, must be prepared, and must be resolved upon the 5th of the following chord.

4. The root of the chord may only be sounded in the bass, and is consequently omitted in all the inversions.

5. The rest of the notes bear the same treatment as in the chord of the 7th, save that the 5th (which, if placed below the 9th, stands at the interval of a 5th from this note) requires to be written with care, to prevent the part in which it stands from proceeding in 5ths with that which has the 9th. To avoid such faulty progression, the 5th may rise to the 3rd of the following chord :—

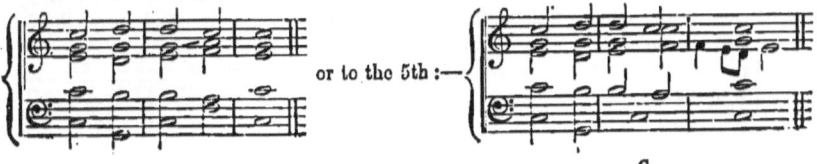

or to the 5th :—

G

or, being placed above the 9th, it may proceed in 4ths with this note:—

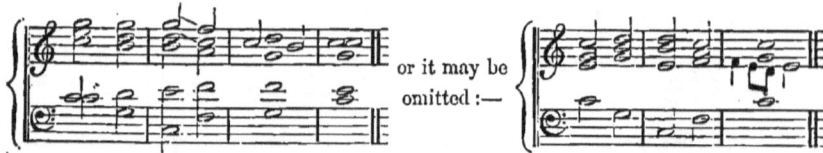

or it may be omitted:—

6. The chord of the 9th, having four notes besides the root, has four inversions; the last inversion, however, is unavailable. As the root of the chord of the 9th is omitted in all the inversions (Chap. XI. sect. 4), the first inversion of this chord consists of the same intervals as the chord of the 7th, in its original position; the second inversion of the 9th, of the same as the first inversion of the chord of the 7th; and the third inversion of the chord of the 9th, of the same as the second inversion of the chord of the 7th: the inversions of the chord of the 9th are distinguished from those of the chord of the 7th, by their resolution. This combination of notes, however approached, may be resolved either as a complete chord of the 7th (direct or inverted), or as a chord of the 9th with the root omitted (Chap. X. sect. 4):—

7. When the root of the chord of the 9th is omitted, the 7th (except when it is the bass-note) ceases to be a dissonance, and therefore needs neither preparation nor resolution. When, however, the 7th of the chord (being the leading-note or the subdominant) forms a dissonance with the 3rd of the chord, the rules for its preparation and resolution must be observed. †

8. The first inversion of the chord of the 9th has the 3rd in the bass; the 9th is then the 7th to the bass, the 7th is the 5th to the bass, and the 5th is the 3rd to the bass:—

9. The second inversion of the chord of the 9th has the 5th in the bass, and it must be resolved upon a first inversion of a chord on the note next above. The 9th is then the 5th to the bass, the 7th is the 3rd to the bass, and the 3rd is the 6th to the bass:—

10. The third inversion of the chord of the 9th has the 7th in the bass (which, being a dissonance with the 4th above it, must be prepared), and it must be resolved on the first inversion of a chord on the note next below. The 9th is then the 3rd to the bass, the 5th is the 6th to the bass, and the 3rd is the 4th to the bass:—

---

* Not available as the second inversion of a chord of the 7th (Chap. X. sect. 4).
† Appendix Y.

11. The chord of the 9th on the 3rd degree of the major or minor key, when the root is omitted, appears as the chord of the dominant 7th; and the resolution of this upon the chord of the submediant is a progression so common, that it is frequently regarded as an exceptional treatment of the dominant harmony. Whenever the chord of the dominant 7th is employed, it may either be resolved (according to its own rule) upon the chord of the key-note, or (according to this rule) upon a chord of which the 6th degree of the key is the root (Chap. X. sect. 12) :—

THE DOMINANT MINOR 9TH.

12. The chord of the minor 9th on the dominant may be taken without preparation in either the minor or major key, being diatonic in the former, and chromatic in the latter.

13. This chord consists of the chord of the dominant 7th (Chap. X. sect. 13) with a minor 9th added to it :—

14. The 9th may be resolved (after the manner of a suspended discord), while the rest of the chord remains; or it may be resolved with the rest of the chord upon a chord having another root :—

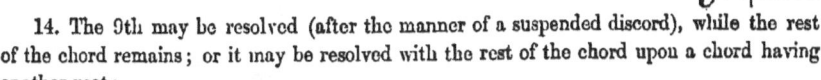

15. If resolved while the rest of the chord remains, the 9th may proceed either to the root or to the 3rd of the chord :—

Resolved on the Root of the same Chord.

16. If the 9th resolve upon the root of the same chord, the root should not (save in some very rare cases) be sounded in any of the upper parts together with the 9th; the root is consequently omitted in all the inversions of the chord.

17. In this form, the chord of the dominant 9th may be employed in all its four inversions.

18. The first inversion has the 3rd in the bass, when the 9th and root are successively the 7th and 6th to the bass :—

19. The second inversion has the 5th in the bass, when the 9th and root are successively the 5th and 4th to the bass :—

20. The third inversion has the 7th in the bass, when the 9th and root are successively the 3rd and 2nd to the bass :—‡

21. The last inversion has the 9th in the bass, which is accompanied with the 2nd, 4th, and 6th, and these remain as the 3rd 5th, and 7th, when the bass is resolved :—

Resolved on the 3rd of the same Chord.

22. If the 9th resolve upon the 3rd of the same chord, it may either rise a 2nd, or fall a 7th to its resolution :—

23. When the 9th is thus resolved, the 3rd must not, in any of the parts, be sounded together with the 9th; but the root and 7th should both be sounded with the 9th (Chap. XI. sect. 25).

24. As the 3rd may not be sounded, the first inversion of the chord in this form is unavailable. The other three inversions are but rarely employed.

25. When the 9th is resolved upon the 3rd of the same chord, the root may be taken instead of the 7th; and then it must proceed to the 7th, at the same time as the 9th proceeds to the 3rd :—

Resolved on a Chord derived from another Root.-

26. If the 9th resolve with the rest of the chord, the chord of the dominant 9th must be resolved upon the chord of the key-note, and the 9th must fall to the 5th of the following chord :—*

27. Under this treatment of the chord the root may not appear in any part but the bass, and is consequently omitted in all the inversions. The first inversion, therefore, consists of the leading-note with its 3rd, 5th, and 7th, which last being a diminished 7th, the combination is often called the "chord of the diminished 7th," its derivation from the real root being disregarded:—

28. In resolving the last inversion, care must be taken that the 4th to the bass (the 5th of the original chord) proceed not to the root of the next chord, progressing thus in 4ths with the bass (Chap. III. sect. 12) :—

to avoid this fault, the 4th should rise either to the 3rd or 5th of the following chord :—†

* Appendix M.   ‡ Appendix S.

† In the third inversion, the 7th (being the bass) sometimes leaps downward to the key-note, the root
of the next chord, when the 5th in the chord of the 9th goes to the 3rd of the key-note.

The Dominant Major 9th.

29. A chord of the major 9th on the dominant may be taken without preparation, but in the major key only.

30. This chord consists of the chord of the dominant 7th with a major 9th added to it :—

31. The 9th may be resolved on the root or the 3rd, while the rest of the chord remains; or it may be resolved on a chord having another root.

Resolved on the Root of the same Chord.

32. The root may not be sounded in any of the upper parts together with the 9th; it is consequently omitted in all the inversions of the chord, until it appears as the resolution of the 9th :—

33. The major 9th should not be sounded below the 3rd, and it cannot, therefore, when resolved upon the root, be employed in the bass; the last inversion of the chord is consequently unavailable.

34. In other respects, the rules for the resolution of the minor 9th upon the root apply also to the major 9th (Chap. XI. sects. 16 to 21).

Resolved on the 3rd of the same Chord.

35. The rules for the resolution of the minor 9th upon the 3rd of the same chord apply also to the major 9th (Chap. XI. sects. 22 to 25); except that the inversions of the chord with the major 9th are more frequently employed than those of the chord with the minor 9th :—

Resolved on a Chord derived from another Root.

36. The chord of the major 9th on the dominant is resolved upon the chord of the key-note, when the 9th falls to the 5th of the following chord :—*

37. The root is omitted in all the inversions. The major 9th *should* not be sounded below the 3rd, and thus the last inversion is unavailable :—

* Appendix M.

THE SUPERTONIC MINOR 9TH.

38. A chromatic chord of the minor 9th on the supertonic may be taken without preparation, in either the minor or major key.

39. This chord consists of the chromatic chord of the 7th on the supertonic (Chap. X. sect. 21), with the addition of the minor 9th; and its intervals are thus the same as those of the chord of the dominant minor 9th :—

40. As in the dominant chord, the 9th may be resolved on the root or the 3rd of the same chord; or it may be resolved on a chord derived from another root.

41. If resolved on the root or the 3rd of the same chord, the supertonic minor 9th follows all the same rules as the dominant minor 9th (Chap. XI. sects. 16 to 25).

42. If resolved on a chord derived from another root, the supertonic minor 9th (like the chromatic common chord and chord of the 7th on the same note) must be followed either by a dominant discord, or by an inversion of the chord of the key-note :—

43. The 9th in this chord must either fall a 2nd (as in other chords of the 9th), or remain to be a note of the next chord :—

or rise a chromatic semitone :—

.•. *In the inversions of this chord, the minor 9th is sometimes written as a chromatic semitone above the root* (Chap. II. sect. 24) :—

THE SUPERTONIC MAJOR 9TH.

44. The chromatic chord of the major 9th on the supertonic may be taken without preparation, but in the major key only.

45. This chord consists of the chromatic chord of the 7th  on the supertonic, with the addition of the major 9th :—

and its intervals, therefore, are the same as those of the chord of the dominant major 9th.

46. The 9th may be resolved while the rest of the chord remains, according to the rules for resolving the dominant major 9th (Chap. XI. sects. 31 to 35).

47. If resolved on a chord derived from another root, the same rule applies to this chord as to the supertonic minor 9th (Chap. XI. sect. 42).

48. The 9th must either fall a 2nd (as in other chords of the 9th), or remain to be a rote of the next chord :—

49. The rule for the omission of the root, and for the relative position of the 3rd and major 9th of the dominant (Chap. XI. sect. 37), applies also to this chord, which has also the same available inversions :—

THE TONIC MINOR 9TH.

50. The chromatic chord of the minor 9th on the key-note may be taken without preparation, in either the minor or major key.

51. This chord consists of the chromatic chord of the 7th on the key-note (Chap. X. sect. 29), with the addition of a minor 9th (which is always chromatic), and its intervals are thus the same as those of the chord of the dominant minor 9th :—

52. As in the dominant and supertonic chords, the 9th may be resolved on the root or the 3rd of the same chord; or it may be resolved on a chord derived from another root.

53. If resolved on the root or the 3rd of the same chord, the tonic minor 9th follows all the same rules as the dominant minor 9th (Chap. XI. sects. 16 to 25).

54. If resolved on a chord derived from another root, the tonic minor 9th (like the chromatic chord of the 7th on the same note) must be followed by a dominant discord, or by a supertonic discord :—*

55. The 9th in this chord must either rise a chromatic semitone, or it may fall a 2nd, provided the root be not retained as a note of the following chord (*see Examples to Sect.* 54).

THE TONIC MAJOR 9TH.

56. The chromatic chord of the major 9th may be taken on the key-note without preparation, in either the major or minor key.

57. This chord consists of the chromatic chord of the 7th on the key-note, with the addition of the major 9th:— and its intervals are thus the same as those of the chord of the dominant major 9th.

58. The 9th may be resolved while the rest of the chord remains, according to the rules for resolving the dominant major 9th (Chap. XI. sects. 31 to 35).

59. If resolved on a chord derived from another root, the same rule applies to this chord as to the tonic minor 9th (Chap. XI. sect. 54).*

60. The 9th must then either remain to be a note of the next chord :—

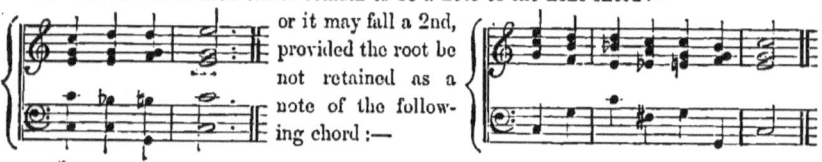

or it may fall a 2nd, provided the root be not retained as a note of the following chord :—

CHAPTER XII.

CHORD OF THE ELEVENTH.

1. THE chord of the 11th on the dominant may be taken without preparation.

2. This chord consists of either the chord of the minor 9th, or the major 9th on the dominant with the addition of an 11th,—but either the 3rd or the 5th must be omitted when the 11th is sounded :—

3. The 11th may be resolved (like the 9th), while the rest of the chord remains :—

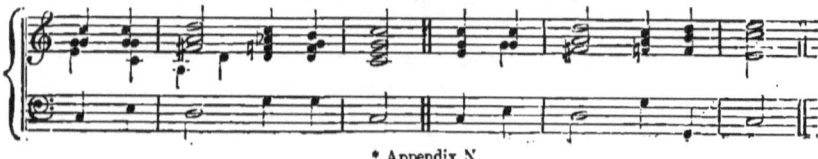

* Appendix N.

or it may be resolved (also like the 9th) *with* the rest of the chord, upon a chord having another root :—

4. If resolved while the rest of the chord remains, the 11th may be resolved either upon the 3rd, or upon the 5th of the chord.

Resolved on the 3rd of the same Chord.

5. If the 11th resolve upon the 3rd, the 3rd must in no case be sounded together with the 11th. In this form the 11th somewhat resembles the suspended 4th; but it differs from that discord in so much as it needs not preparation; and in so much as, when the 11th is resolved, there should still remain one or more dissonant  notes of the dominant harmony, if in the last case the root be sounded with the 11th.*

6. When the root is omitted (Chap. XI. sect. 16), as well as the 3rd, the 7th ceases to be a dissonant note, and thus in all the inversions of this form of the chord, the 7th is free in its progression.

7. The first available inversion has the 5th in the bass, when the 11th is the 7th to the bass, the 9th is either the diminished or the perfect 5th to the bass (according as it is the minor or the major 9th), and the 7th is the 3rd to the bass. The bass of this inversion may either remain, or rise to the root, when the 11th and the 9th are resolved :—

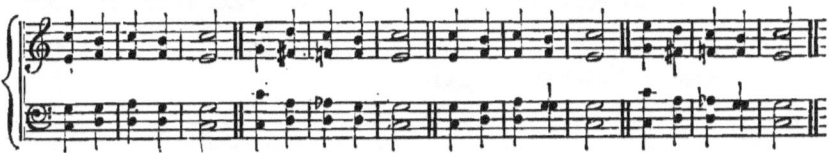

8. The next inversion has the 7th in the bass, when the 11th, 9th, and 5th of the original chord are the 5th, 3rd, and 6th to the bass. In this form the chord is named by some theorists "the chord of the added 6th" :—

9. The next inversion has the 9th in the bass, when the 11th, 7th, and 5th of the original chord are the 3rd, 6th, and 4th to the bass. When the 9th is major, this inversion can rarely be used with good effect :

10. The last inversion has the 11th in the bass, when the 9th, 7th, and 5th of the original chord are the 6th, 4th, and 2nd to the bass :—

Resolved on the 5th of the same Chord.

11. If the 11th resolve on the 5th of the same chord, the 5th may not, except in one instance (Chap. XII. sect. 16) be sounded together with the 11th.

12. The 3rd *may* be sounded together with the 11th, but this form of the chord is rarely employed :—

13. It is more common for the 9th to rise to the 3rd, when the 11th rises to the 5th. In this form of the chord, the root and the 7th must be sounded, the 3rd and the 5th must be omitted :—

14. The first available inversion has the 7th in the bass, when the 11th, 9th, and root are the 5th, 3rd, and 2nd to the bass :—

15. The only other available inversion has the 9th in the bass, when the 11th, 7th, and root are the 3rd, 6th, and 7th to the bass :—

16. This form of the chord may also be taken with the 5th in the bass, provided such bass-note descend to the root when the 11th and 9th proceed to the 5th and 3rd :—

17. When the 11th and 9th proceed to the 5th and 3rd, the root may be taken instead of the 7th, and then it must fall to the 7th at the same time as the 9th and the 11th are resolved (Chap. XI. sect. 25) :—

Resolved on a Chord derived from another Root.

18. If the 11th be resolved with the rest of the chord, the chord may be resolved upon the chord of the key-note, or upon a supertonic discord.

19. In this form of the chord, the root can only be sounded in the bass; the 3rd must always be omitted: the 5th must not descend to that note in the following chord which was the 11th in this (Chap. III. sect. 17); and the 7th may fall a 2nd, or rise a chromatic semitone,—and, when the root is omitted, it is free to rise a 2nd, to fall a 4th, or rise a 5th (Chap. XII. sect. 6).

20. The first available inversion has the 5th in the bass:—

21. The next inversion has the 7th in the bass:—

22. The next inversion has the minor 9th in the bass:—

23. The last inversion has the 11th in the bass :—

CHAPTER XIII.

CHORDS OF THE THIRTEENTH.

THE DOMINANT MINOR 13TH.

1. A CHORD of the minor 13th on the dominant may be taken without preparation.

2. This chord consists of the chord of the dominant 11th (Chap. XII. sect. 2), with the addition of the minor 13th :— 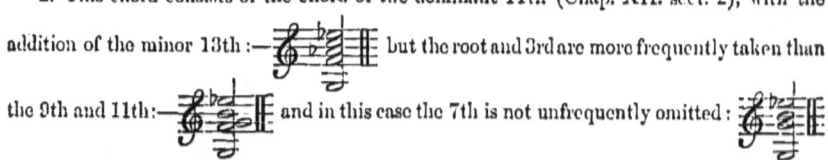 but the root and 3rd are more frequently taken than the 9th and 11th :— and in this case the 7th is not unfrequently omitted :—

3. The 13th (like the 9th and the 11th) may be resolved, while the rest of the chord remains; or it may be resolved (also like the 9th and the 11th) with the rest of the chord, upon a chord having another root :—

4. If resolved while the rest of the chord remains, the minor 13th on the dominant can only be employed in the minor key; the 13th may be resolved either upon the 5th or upon the 7th of the chord.

Resolved upon the 5th of the same Chord.

5. If the 13th resolve upon the 5th, the 5th must not be sounded together with the 13th, and the 13th should not be sounded below the 7th :—

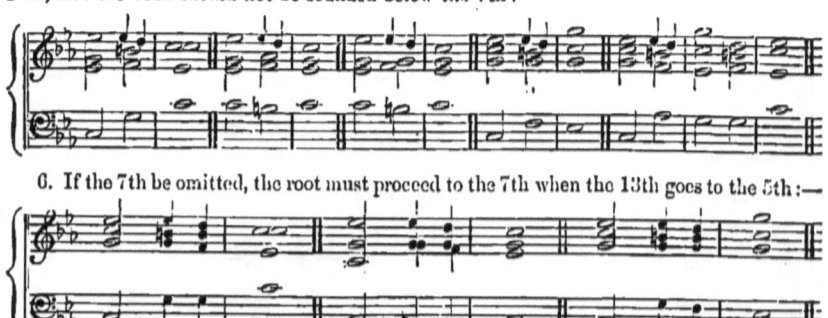

6. If the 7th be omitted, the root must proceed to the 7th when the 13th goes to the 5th :—

7. If the root, the 3rd, and the 5th be omitted, this chord appears as a chord of the 7th on the subdominant, the 13th being the 7th to the bass,—the 11th the 5th to the bass,— and the 9th the 3rd to the bass. The bass, which is the 7th of the original chord, is then free in its progression (Chap. XII. sect. 6):—

Resolved on the 7th of the same Chord.

8. If the 13th resolve upon the 7th, the 7th must not be sounded together with the 13th:—

Resolved on a Chord derived from another Root.

9. The chord of the minor 13th on the dominant is resolved upon the chord of the key-note; it may be employed in both the minor and the major key.‡

10. The 13th may remain to be the minor 3rd of the following chord, when the 7th may not be sounded together with the 13th (Chap. III. sect. 17) :*—

or it may rise a chromatic semitone to the major 3rd of the following chord :—

₊ *In this latter case it is more common to write the minor 13th as an augmented 5th to the root* (Chap. II. sect. 24) :†—

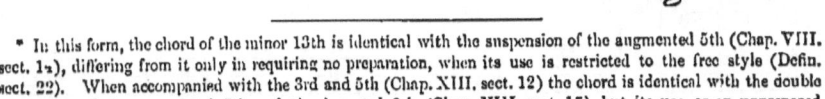

---

* In this form, the chord of the minor 13th is identical with the suspension of the augmented 5th (Chap. VIII. sect. 1₂), differing from it only in requiring no preparation, when its use is restricted to the free style (Defin. sect. 22). When accompanied with the 3rd and 5th (Chap. XIII. sect. 12) the chord is identical with the double suspension of the augmented 5th and the inverted 9th (Chap. VIII. sect. 17), but its use, as an unprepared discord, is restricted to the free style.

† In this form, the chord of the minor 13th (as thus frequently written) resembles the chord of the augmented 5th on the mediant of the key of E minor (Chap. IX. sect. 4); but it differs from that chord in requiring no preparation; in never having its 3rd doubled, because this is the leading-note; in being accompanied with the minor 7th, whereas the diatonic discord may be accompanied with the major 7th (Chap. X. sect. 7); and in being resolved upon the chord of the key-note, whereas that chord is resolved upon the chord of the submediant. However familiar the chord of the minor 13th may be with this notation, and however expedient may be the use of this notation on account of such familiarity, there are sufficient examples, in the works of the great masters, of the note written as a 13th, and not as a 5th to the root, to prove their belief in its fundamental origin. The naming of the note is of secondary importance, but the knowledge of its derivation is essential to a clear idea of its treatment. I refer musicians for unanswerable arguments on this subject, and on that of the chord of the 11th, to the "Treatise on Harmony" of Alfred Day.—*Harrison & Co.*

‡ Appendix M.

11. The minor 13th may be accompanied with the root and 3rd only :—

12. The minor 13th may be accompanied with the root, 3rd, and 5th, but it is then mostly employed in the last inversion, having the 13th for the bass :—

13. The minor 13th may be accompanied with the root, 3rd, and 7th, when it must be sounded above the 7th. In this form it can only be employed in the major key (Chap. XIII. sect. 10).

14. The minor 13th may be accompanied with the minor or major 9th, in addition to the intervals last described :—

15. The 13th (however accompanied, except when the 5th is sounded against it), may leap a 3rd to the root of the following chord, if this chord be minor :—

The Dominant Major 13th.

16. A chord of the major 13th on the dominant may be taken without preparation in the major key only.

17. This chord consists of the same intervals as that of the minor 13th, except that the 13th is major instead of minor. (Chap. XIII. sect. 2):—

18. The major 13th may resolve like the minor 13th, on the 5th or on the 7th of the same chord (Chap. XIII. sects. 5 to 8) :—

19. The chord of the major 13th on the dominant may be resolved on the chord of the key-note; when the 13th must leap a 3rd to the root of the following chord:—*

The Supertonic Minor 13th.†

20. A chord of the minor 13th on the supertonic may be taken without preparation in both the major and minor key.

21. This chord consists of the chord of the minor or major 9th on the same note (Chap. XI. sects. 39 and 45), with the addition of the minor 13th; but any of the notes, except the 13th and the 3rd, may be omitted.

22. The 13th of the supertonic is rarely resolved while the rest of the chord remains.

23. The chord of the minor 13th on the supertonic is resolved upon a dominant discord or upon a tonic discord.

24. If the chord resolve upon a dominant discord, the 13th rises a chromatic semitone to the 3rd of the following chord. In this case the 7th must be omitted (since its resolution would induce the doubling of the leading-note) (Chap. IV. sect. 3); the 5th is rarely employed; and it is not desirable to have the 9th in the chord:—

25. If the chord resolve upon a tonic discord, the 13th remains to be the 7th of the following chord:—

* Appendix M.   † See Appendix W.

The Tonic Minor 13th.

26. A chord of the minor 13th on the key-note may be taken without preparation in both the major and minor key.

27. This chord consists of the chord of the minor or major 9th on the same note (Chap. XI. sects. 51 and 57), with the addition of the minor 13th.

28. The 13th may resolve on the 5th or on the 7th of the same chord, according to the same rules as the dominant 13th (Chap. XIII. sects. 5 to 8).

29. The chord of the minor 13th on the key-note is resolved upon a dominant discord, or upon a supertonic discord.*

30. If the chord resolve upon a dominant discord, the 13th may fall a 2nd to the root of the next chord :—

or remain to be the minor 9th of the next chord :

or rise a chromatic semitone to the major 9th of the next chord, provided the 7th be not sounded together with the 13th (Chap. III. sect. 15) :—

31. If the chord resolve upon a supertonic discord, the 13th must rise a chromatic semitone to the 5th of the next chord :—

The Tonic Major 13th.

32. A chord of the major 13th on the key-note may be taken, without preparation, in the major key only.

33. This chord consists of the chord of the minor or major 9th on the same note (Chap. XI. sects. 51 and 57), with the addition of the major 13th.

34. The 13th may resolve on the 5th or on the 7th, according to the same rules as the dominant 13th (Chap. XIII. sect. 18).

35. The chord of the major 13th on the key-note is resolved upon a dominant discord; when the 13th may fall a 2nd, to the root of the next chord :—*

or it may fall a chromatic semitone to the minor 9th of the next chord :—

or it may remain to be the major 9th of the next chord :—

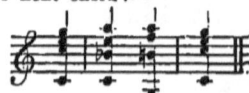

* Appendix ♪

CHAPTER XIV.

CHORDS OF THE AUGMENTED SIXTH.

1. A CHORD of the augmented 6th may be taken without preparation, on the minor 6th of the key.

2. This chord consists of the minor 9th of the dominant with the major 3rd and the 7th of the supertonic,—to which either the root or the minor 9th of this latter chromatic chord may be added :—*

3. This chord is resolved upon the common-chord of the dominant or its first inversion; or on the common chord of the key-note or one of its inversions; or on an inversion of the dominant minor 9th; or upon a supertonic discord. The first two of these resolutions are those most frequently employed :—

4. The two notes which form the interval of the augmented 6th, must never proceed in similar motion with each other. With this restriction all the notes of this compound chord

* Appendix R.

I

proceed according to the rules for the treatment of the two chords, the notes of which are here combined (Chap. XI. sects. 12 to 28, and 38 to 43). Thus the lower note of the augmented 6th (the dominant minor 9th) may fall a 2nd to the root or the 5th of a chord; or may remain as a 9th, when the notes peculiar to the supertonic are resolved; or may rise a chromatic semitone to the 5th of the supertonic :—

the upper note of the augmented 6th (the major 3rd of the supertonic) may rise a 2nd to the root or the 5th of a chord, or may fall a chromatic semitone to the 7th in the chord of the dominant 9th; or may remain as a 3rd when the note peculiar to the dominant is resolved :—

the 3rd to the bass (the supertonic 7th) may fall a 2nd to the 3rd of the dominant; and, if doubled, may also rise a 2nd :—

or may remain to be the root of the chord of the key-note; and if doubled may also rise a 3rd or a 5th :—

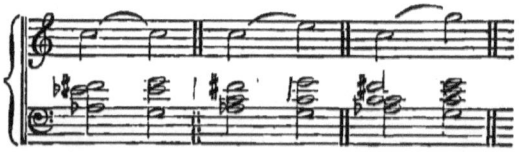

the 4th to the bass (the supertonic) may remain, or may rise a 2nd or a 4th :—

the 5th to the bass (the supertonic minor 9th) may remain, or may rise a chromatic semitone, or (provided it proceed not in 5ths with the bass) may fall a 2nd :—

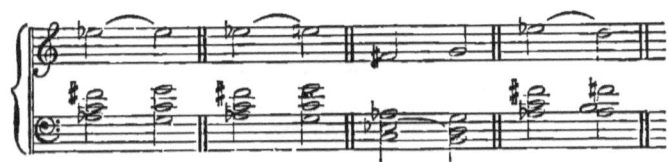

5. The two notes which form the augmented 6th are most rarely inverted as a diminished 3rd. The other notes of the chord may be placed in any position, and thus the chord may have two inversions, the last of which varies according to whether the root or the minor 9th of the supertonic be employed :—

6. A chord of the augmented 6th may also be, but is much more rarely, taken without preparation on the minor 2nd of the key, with the restriction that, in the minor key, it may not be resolved on the common chord of the key-note.

7. This chord consists of the minor 9th of the tonic, with the 3rd and 7th of the dominant,—to which either the root or the minor 9th of this latter chord may be added. The progression of all these notes is similar to that of the corresponding notes in the chord of the augmented 6th on the minor 6th of the key :—*

* Appendix R.

CHAPTER XV.

MODULATION.

1. In the diatonic style, Modulation is effected by any chord containing a note foreign to the key that is to be quitted. It is desirable that the chord which changes the key should be either one with its root in the bass, or a first inversion on the 2nd of the new key (Chap. IV. sect. 17). This passage—

is therefore preferable to this one :—

2. Great care should be taken in compositions in a minor key, not to confound this with the relative major by the employment of chords peculiar to the latter without completely confirming the modulation. Such confusion of keys occurs in these passages :—

but is avoided in these :—

3. In the free or chromatic style, it has been shown that certain chromatic chords may be employed, which, if they proceed to chords characteristic of the original key, induce no modulation ; on the other hand, change of key may be effected by any concord or discord containing notes foreign to the key that is to be quitted, either in the original position or in any available inversion.

4. Any of the chromatic concords of the minor or major key, approached as such, may be regarded as characteristic chords of a new key, and quitted accordingly.

5. Any major common chord may be regarded as the chromatic concord on the minor 2nd, or as that on the minor 6th of the key, and quitted accordingly.

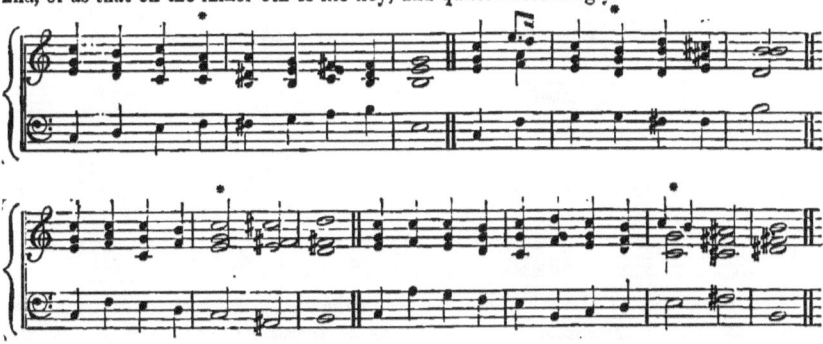

6. In modulating to the minor key of the 2nd of the original key, it is desirable (except the tonic of the first key rise a chromatic semitone to the leading-note of the second key) to have a chord containing the minor 6th of the key that is approached, before introducing the common chord of the dominant :—

rather than thus—

7. The several chromatic harmonies of the supertonic and the tonic having the same intervals as the harmonies of the dominant, any of these chords may be approached as belonging to either one of the three roots, and quitted as belonging to either of the other two; thus the dominant of one key may be regarded as the supertonic or the tonic of another key,—the supertonic of one key may be regarded as the dominant or the tonic of another, &c.

8. The resolutions that have been described of the fundamental discords, prove them all to be available in any one key; such resolutions, as regards the *chords* to which these discords proceed in the same key, are to be considered the natural resolutions. If, however, the several *notes* make their proper progression, each of the fundamental discords may proceed to some chord out of the key, and so be resolved in a different key from that in which it is approached. The proper progressions of the notes of the fundamental discords are as follows :— The 3rd must rise a 2nd, or remain, or fall a chromatic semitone :—

The 7th must fall a 2nd, or remain, or rise a chromatic semitone :—

The minor 9th must fall a 2nd, or remain, or rise a chromatic semitone :—

The major 9th must fall a 2nd, or remain, or fall a chromatic semitone :—

The 11th must remain :—

The minor 13th must fall a 2nd, or remain, or rise a chromatic semitone :—

The major 13th must fall a 2nd, or remain, or fall a chromatic semitone :—*

9. Modulation may be made from a key with flats to a key with sharps, or the reverse, by the enharmonic change of notation.

10. The inversions of the chord of the minor 9th (in which the root must be omitted), may, according to the notation, belong to either of four roots :—

* Appendix M.

Each of these four roots may be a dominant, a supertonic, or a tonic, and may so belong to either of three major or minor keys. This one combination may thus by enharmonic change of notation induce a modulation to any of the twelve major or twelve minor keys:—

11. Any note of a fundamental discord may remain to be any other note of any other fundamental discord; that is, the root of an unprepared chord of the 7th may remain, to be

the 3rd, or the 5th, or the 7th, or the minor 9th, or the major 9th, or the 11th, or the minor 13th, or the major 13th of another chord :—

and the same is the case with the 3rd, the 5th, the 7th, &c.

CONCLUSION.

The student is recommended habitually to analyse music by the rules given throughout this book, which is designed to be a guide in the best field of study,—the music of the greatest composers.

The subject of this book is more fully discussed in the Author's "Six Lectures on Harmony."—*Longman & Co.*; "Counterpoint."—*Cambridge Warehouse;* "Eighty Musical Sentences."—*Cramer & Co.;* and most of all in "A Treatise on Harmony," by Alfred Day.—*Harrison & Co.*

PROGRESSIVE EXERCISES,

DESIGNED AS MODELS, ACCORDING TO WHICH THE STUDENT SHOULD CONSTRUCT OTHERS OF HIS OWN.

CHAPTER I. TO SECTION 15.

THE student should construct several tables of intervals, reckoning the intervals from other notes, as, in the table given in this chapter, they are reckoned from C.

EXERCISE ON INTERVALS.—The student should mark over each interval its name and quality (as major 2nd, perfect 5th, &c.) and the number of semitones it contains.

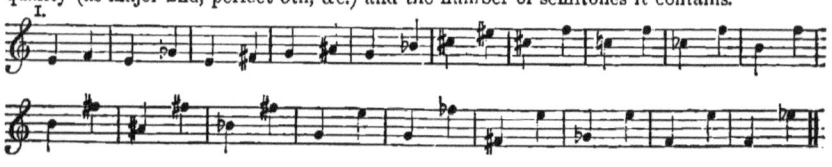

CHAPTER II. TO SECTION 13.

The student should construct scales in several major keys, marking no signature, but placing the sharps or flats before the proper notes, so as to induce the correct arrangement of the notes with reference to the key-note, and the consequently correct position of the semitones and tones; thus—

CHAPTER IV. TO SECTION 9.

EXERCISES to be written in four parts and in score.   (Definitions, sect. 4).
EXPLANATION.—Each bass note is the root of a common chord.

Chapter II. to Section 19.

The student should write scales in several minor keys, marking the signature of the relative major key, and placing the accidental sharp or natural before the leading-note where it occurs; thus—

Chapter IV. to Section 13.

Exercises to be written in four parts and in score.

Explanation.—A natural, sharp, or flat over or under a bass-note signifies that the 3rd of such note is to be natural, sharp, or flat, and to be so marked in the part where it occurs.

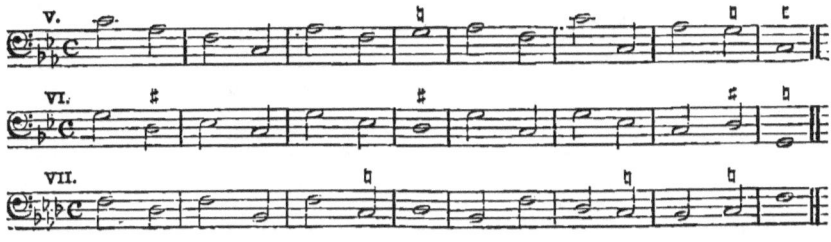

Chapter IV. to Section 20.

Exercises to be written in four parts.

Explanation.—When the figure 6 is marked over or under a bass-note, it signifies that such note bears a 1st inversion.

Chapter IV. to Section 25.

Explanation.—A sharp, flat, or natural, before any figure, signifies that the note represented by such figure is to be sharp, flat, or natural; thus, ♮6 over D signifies that B natural is to be written as the 6th of D. Some put a line through, instead of a ♯ before a figure 6.

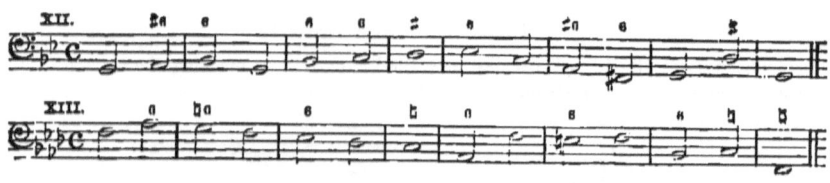

CHAPTER IV. TO SECTION 31.

EXPLANATION.—The figures $\frac{6}{4}$ over or under a bass-note, signify that such note bears a 2nd inversion. The figures $\frac{5}{3}$ are employed to contradict any previous figuring on the same note. Two sets of figures over one bass-note, signify that the time of the upper parts is to be divided between the two chords indicated by such figures.

CHAPTER V. TO SECTION 5.

The student should write exercises of his own on common chords and 1st and 2nd inversions, introducing examples of dominant and tonic pedals; and in exercises on subjects subsequently explained, it will be desirable also occasionally to exemplify the employment of pedals.

CHAPTER VI. TO SECTION 5.

The student should write exercises on ascending and on descending sequences; at first making the original progression consist of two chords; afterwards making the original progression consist of three or more chords.

Chapter VII. to Section 3

Exercises on passing-notes, some of which are in the bass, and others should be introduced in the upper parts when they can be properly approached and quitted.

Explanation.—A line over or under several notes, signifies that the chord belonging to the first of such notes is to be retained or repeated so long as the line continues. A line drawn from any figure signifies that the chord or the note in a chord, indicated by such figure, is to be retained so long as the line continues.

Chapter II. Sections 20 to 23.

The student should write the arbitrary minor scale in several minor keys, marking the signature of the relative major key, placing the accidental sharps or naturals before the 6th and 7th in ascending, and contradicting these in descending; thus:--

Chapter VII. to Section 5.

Chapter VII. Section 6.

Chapter VIII. Section 6.

EXPLANATION.—The figures 9 8 signify the suspension of the 9th and its resolution; the part that contains which must have two notes equivalent in time to the longer notes of the three other parts.

Chapter VIII. Section 7.

EXPLANATION.—The figures 7 6 signify the first inversion of the suspended 9th and its resolution.

Chapter VIII. Section 8.

EXPLANATION.—The figures $\frac{6}{5}$ $\frac{}{4}$ signify the second inversion of a suspended 9th and its resolution, the line from the 6 denoting that the note indicated by this figure is to be retained while the 5th proceeds to the 4th.

Chapter VIII. Section 9.

EXPLANATION.—The figures $\frac{4}{2}$ signify the last inversion of a suspended 9th; and the lines drawn from these denote that the chord is to be retained until the resolution of the bass on the next note. The figures $\frac{7}{4}$— signify that the root of the chord is to be included in the upper parts.

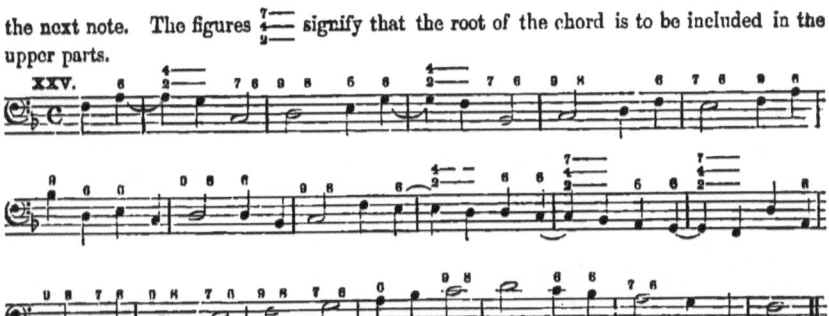

CHAPTER VIII. SECTION 10.

EXPLANATION.—The figures 4 3, or $\frac{5}{4}$ 3, signify the suspension of the 4th and its resolution.

CHAPTER VIII. SECTION 11.

EXPLANATION.—The figures $\frac{9}{6}$—$\frac{8}{6}$ signify the first inversion of the suspended 4th and its resolution.

CHAPTER VIII. SECTION 12.

EXPLANATION.—The figures $\frac{7}{4}$—^{6} signify the second inversion of the suspended 4th and its resolution.

Chapter VIII. Section 13.

EXPLANATION.—The figures $\frac{5}{2}$ signify the last inversion of the suspended 4th; and the lines drawn from these denote that the chord is to be retained until the resolution of the bass on the next note.

Chapter VIII. Section 14.

EXPLANATION.—The figures 5 6 signify the suspension of the dissonant 5th and its resolution.

Chapter VIII. Section 16.

EXPLANATION.—The figures $\frac{6\ 6}{2}$ signify the inversion of $\frac{9}{4}$ with the 4th in the bass. The figures $\frac{4}{3\ 3}$ signify the inversion of $\frac{9}{4}$ with the 9th in the bass.

Chapter VIII. Section 17.

CHAPTER VIII. SECTION 18.

EXPLANATION.—Lines drawn from one note, or from the figuring of one note, to a second note, signify the suspension of the chord belonging to the first note, over the second; the figures that follow such lines, signify the resolution of the chord.

CHAPTER IX. TO SECTION 4.

EXPLANATION.—The figure 5 with a ♯ or ♮ before it, and no figure after it on the same note, signifies the essential discord of the augmented 5th.

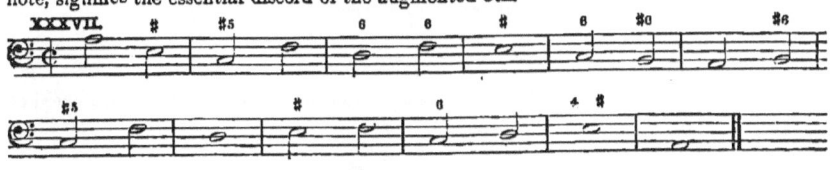

CHAPTER IX. SECTION 5.

EXPLANATION.—The figures ♮/♯ or ♮/♮ over the dominant, signify the first inversion of the augmented 5th.

L

Chapter IX. Section 6.

Explanation.—The figure 5 on the third degree of the major key, denotes the necessity to prepare and resolve the dissonant 5th.

Chapter X. to Section 3.

Explanation.—The figure 7, with no figure after it on the same bass-note, signifies that the bass is the root of a chord of the 7th.

Chapter X. to Section 5.

Explanation.—The figures ⁶₅ signify that the bass bears the first inversion of a chord of the 7th.

* Without the dissonant 5th, which cannot be prepared.

Chapter X. Section 6.

EXPLANATION.—Tho figures $\frac{4}{2}$ or $\frac{6}{4}$ signify that the bass-note bears the third inversion of a chord of the 7th.

Chapter X. Section 7.

Chapter X. Section 8.

Chapter X. Section 9.

L 2

CHAPTER X. SECTION 10.

CHAPTER X. SECTION 11.

The student should write a series of short exercises of his own, exemplifying the chords of the 7th and their inversions on every note of the key; each exercise to begin with the chord of the key-note, introduce the discord to be exemplified, and end with a full close (Definitions, Section 20). To ensure the completeness of this series, it is desirable that the first exercise should exemplify the chord of the 7th on the key-note; the second exercise, the first inversion of this chord; the third exercise, the last inversion; these should be followed by examples of the 7th on the second of the key, the third of the key, &c., throughout the scale; and where a chord of the 7th cannot be used in its original form, its available inversions only should be exemplified. The following are models for such series of exercises in the major and the minor key.

* Appendix O.

CHAPTER X. TO SECTION 20.

EXPLANATION.—The figures $\frac{4}{3}$, or $\frac{6}{4}$, signify that the bass bears the second inversion of a chord of the 7th.

CHAPTER II. SECTIONS 24 TO 27.

The student should write chromatic scales in several minor keys, marking the signature, and placing the accidentals before the notes that require them; thus:—

CHAPTER IV. SECTIONS 32, 33.

Chapter II. Sections 24 to 27.

The student should write chromatic scales in several major keys, marking the signature, and placing the accidentals before the notes that require them; thus:—

Chapter IV. Sections 34, 35.

Chapter XI. to Section 10.

EXPLANATION.—The figures $\frac{9}{7}$, or $\frac{9}{7}$ when the 5th is a discord, denote that the bass is the root of a chord of the 9th. The first inversion of a chord of the 9th is figured like the original position of a chord of the 7th; the second and third inversions of a chord of the 9th are figured like the first and second inversions of a chord of the 7th; the chord which follows shows whether the chord is to be regarded as an inverted chord of the 9th, or as a chord of the 7th.

The student should write a series of short exercises of his own, exemplifying the chords of the 9th and their inversions on every note of the key, upon the same plan as those exemplifying Chapter X. to Section 11. The following will serve as models.

9TH AND 7TH ON THE KEY-NOTE.

9TH AND 7TH ON THE SUPERTONIC.

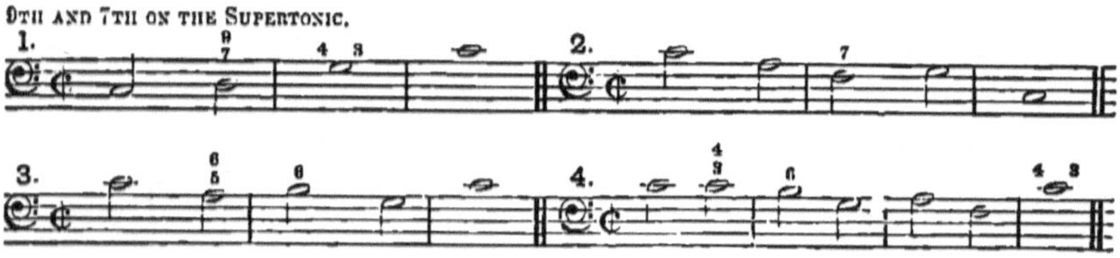

9TH AND 7TH ON THE MEDIANT.

9TH AND 7TH ON THE SUBDOMINANT.

9TH AND 7TH ON THE DOMINANT.

9TH AND 7TH ON THE SUBMEDIANT.

9TH AND 7TH ON THE LEADING-NOTE.

*9TH, 7TH, AND DISSONANT 5TH ON THE SUPERTONIC.

9TH, 7TH, AND DISSONANT 5TH ON THE MEDIANT.

9TH AND 7TH ON THE DOMINANT.

CHAPTER XI. SECTION 11.

* Appendix P.

M

CHAPTER X. SECTIONS 21 TO 27.

CHAPTER X. SECTIONS 28 TO 34.

CHAPTER XI. SECTIONS 16 TO 21.

CHAPTER XI. SECTIONS 22 TO 24.

EXPLANATION.—When the figures are not ranged, as is usual, with the higher numbers above the lower, but have occasionally a lower number above a higher (as 8 above $^6_7$), these figures signify the notes to which those notes should proceed, that are indicated by the figures ranging with them on the same or the previous bass note; thus in the first bar of the next exercise, the 9th of F proceeds to the 3rd, and the 7th remains.

M 2

CHAPTER XI. SECTIONS 36, 37.

CHAPTER XI. SECTIONS 38 TO 43.

CHAPTER XI. SECTIONS 44 TO 49.

CHAPTER XI. SECTIONS 50 TO 55.

CHAPTER XI. SECTIONS 56 TO 60.

CHAPTER XII. TO SECTION 10. *

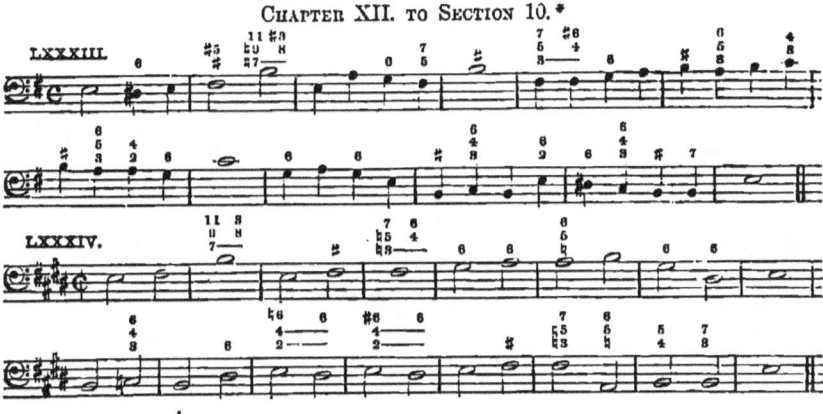

CHAPTER XII. SECTIONS 11 TO 15.

N.B.—It is desirable, when the 11th has been resolved on the 5th of the same root, that the melody, at the next change of harmony, return not to the note which was the 11th, and which, as the discord, was so prominent that its repetition in the melody of the same part would induce an effect of monotony.

CHAPTER XII. SECTION 16.

CHAPTER XII. SECTION 17.

* See Explanation, page 83.

CHAPTER XII. SECTIONS 18 TO 23.

CHAPTER XIII. TO SECTION 6.

CHAPTER XIII. SECTION 7.

CHAPTER XIII. SECTIONS 9 TO 11.

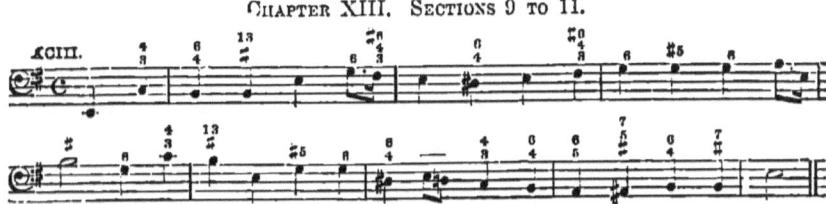

EXPLANATION.—The 13th, when resolved on the major 3rd of another root, is here written as an augmented 5th to the root; the rules against false relation, however (Chapter III. Sections 20 to 24), and every other law for its treatment, refer to the note by its real name, and not by the name under which, in deference to frequent practice, it is here written.

CHAPTER XIII. SECTION 12.

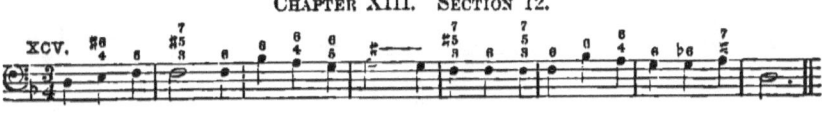

CHAPTER XIII. SECTION 13.

EXPLANATION.—Whatever figures are employed to indicate the 13th and the 7th in the inversions of this chord, and however these figures are ranged, care must be taken to place the 13th above the 7th in the distribution of the parts; thus in the second bar of the next exercise the ♭ 4th (♯ 3rd) of B should be placed higher in the harmony than the 5th of B.

CHAPTER XIII. SECTION 14.

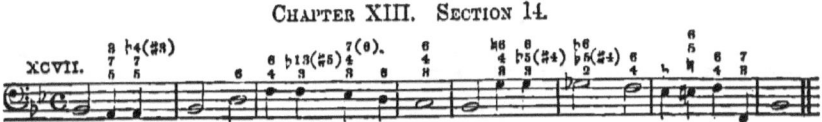

CHAPTER XIII. SECTION 15.

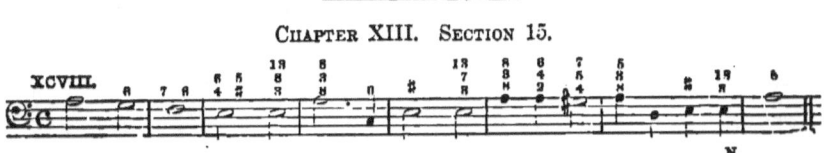

CHAPTER XIII. SECTIONS 16 TO 18.

CHAPTER XIII. SECTIONS 20 TO 25.

CHAPTER XIII. SECTIONS 26 TO 28.

CHAPTER XIII. SECTIONS 29 TO 31.

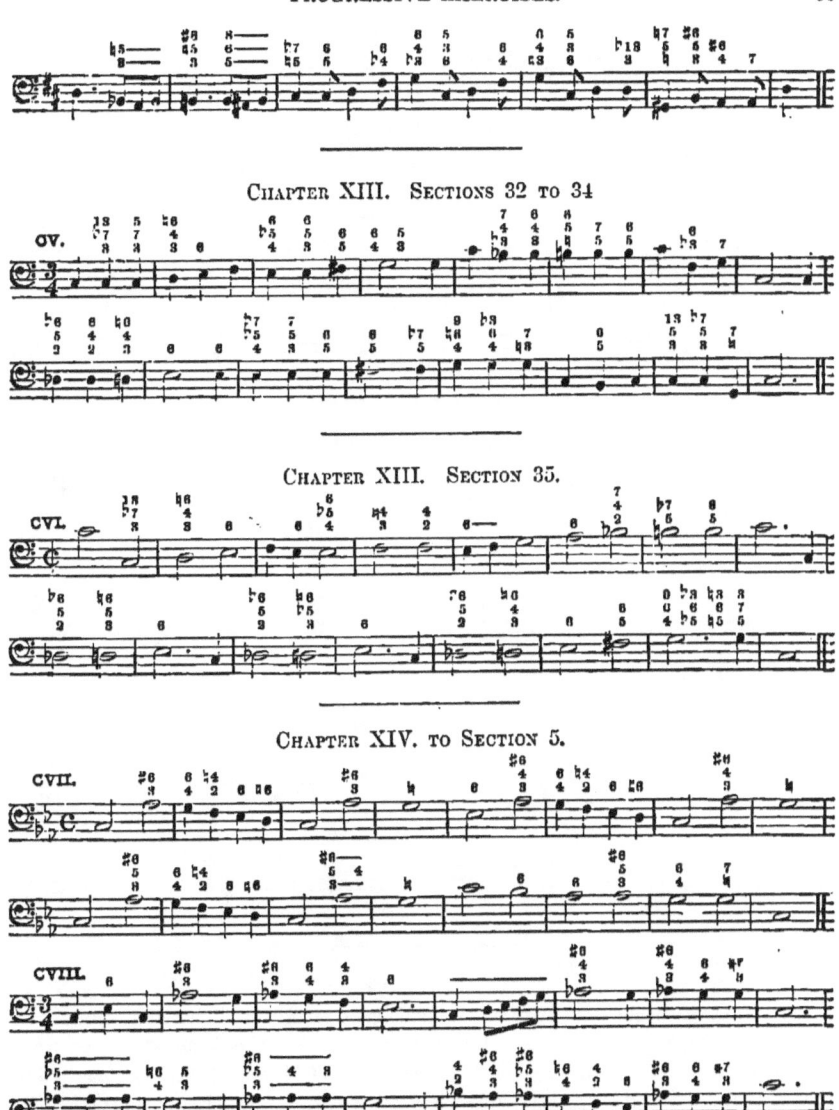

CHAPTER XIII. SECTIONS 32 TO 34

CHAPTER XIII. SECTION 35.

CHAPTER XIV. TO SECTION 5.

EXPLANATION.—Whatever figures are employed to indicate the two notes which form the interval of the augmented 6th in the inversions of the chord, and however these figures are ranged, care must be taken, in the distribution of the parts, that the notes stand at the interval of an augmented 6th from each other, not at that of a diminished 3rd; thus, the ♯4th of C should be placed higher in the harmony than the ♭6th of C.

CHAPTER XIV. SECTION 6.

CHAPTER XV.

The Student should write Exercises on Modulation of his own, illustrating the several rules in this chapter. As the object of such exercises is to practise the art of passing from one key to another, there can be no further model given for them than the examples in this chapter, which would leave any discretion to the fancy and invention of the writer. The end of study is not to fill up the chords upon a given bass, but to invent harmonic progressions; and enough has been already shown to enable the student thus to prove his talent.

APPENDIX.

A.—DEFINITIONS, SECT. 20.—It is necessary in a full close that the dominant harmony, which precedes the final chord, have the root (Def. sect. 7) in the bass :—

The sole exception from this is when the penultimate chord consists of the supertonic, with its 3rd and 6th (Chap. X. sect. 19);

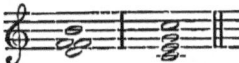

a form of cadence much employed by early writers, but less used now. The close proceeding from a dominant harmony is distinguished by the term *Authentic*, from that proceeding from the subdominant which is called *Plagal*.

B.—CHAP. III. SECT. 9.—It is also good, in approaching a second inversion of a chord, for the extreme parts to proceed downwards in similar motion to an 8th, either by step of a 2nd, or by leap :—

C.—CHAP. III. SECT. 13.—Another exception from the necessary rising of the leading-note in a change of harmony, is when this note is comprised in the second chord, but appears in a different part from that to which it is assigned in the first chord :—

D.—CHAP. III. SECT. 17.—Neither may any part proceed by similar motion to the 8th or unison of the note that resolves a discord, even though coming from any other interval than the 2nd or 7th :—

E.—Chap. III. Sect. 22.—When the chromatic chord of the minor 2nd of the key (Chap. IV. sect. 33), and the chord of the dominant are either of them the first, and the other the third chord in a progression, there is no false relation between the 5th of the one and the root of the other :—

When the first chord is the dominant of a minor key, and the third chord has its root a minor 3rd above it, being either the dominant of the minor 3rd above the original key-note, or being the supertonic of the minor 6th of the original key-note, there also is no false relation :—

F.—Chap. IV. Sect. 32.—The chromatic common chord of the supertonic, or its inversion, may likewise be followed by a chromatic discord of the key-note without disturbing the tonality :—

Change of key is not necessarily involved in the progression of this chord, or of any of the chromatic discords springing from the same root, to a common chord of the dominant, provided the chords immediately following such progression be characteristic of the primary key; but then, the whole phrase must be regarded, rather than the two chords, as maintaining the original tonality. Notable instances of this progression from supertonic to dominant, distinguished from the relationship of dominant and tonic, are when a half close is employed preparatory to the introduction of a new phrase, probably in a different key from that which has previously prevailed.

G.—Chap. IV. Sect. 33.—This chromatic common chord on the minor 2nd of the key is also, though very rarely, taken with good effect in the second inversion :—

H.—Chap. VII. Sects. 4 and 5.—When the leading-note is a harmony-note, the major 6th is used as a passing-note from or to it :—

When the submediant is a harmony-note, the minor 7th is a passing-note from or to it :—

I.—Chap. VII. Sect. 12.—If two parts proceed together in passing-notes, when one steps a semitone that belongs to the diatonic scale of the key, the other may step either a semitone or a tone :—

When one steps a semitone that is induced by chromatic alteration, the other must step a semitone also :—

When two parts proceed in 3rds or 6ths, both having passing-notes, the need does not hold for the note below a root or 5th or 7th to be at the interval of a semitone :—

J.—Chap. VIII. Sect. 1.—The sole exception from this rule is, that the suspended 9th in one chord may be resolved on the 3rd of another chord whose root is at the interval of a 3rd below the root of the suspended 9th ;

but the use of this exception, in exercises at least, may well be deferred till mastery has been gained of the ordinary treatment of suspensions.

K.—Chap. X. Sect. 11.—The 7th on the leading-note may likewise be taken in its first inversion, firstly, if resolved on the last inversion of the mediant 7th ;

and secondly, if resolved on the mediant triad with its 5th duly prepared and resolved:—

L.—THE DOMINANT 7TH, p. 37.—In this and every unprepared discord of which the dominant, supertonic, or the tonic is the root, the discordant notes may be transferred from one part to any other, and must be resolved in that part in which they last appear (Chap. VIII. sect. 15) :—

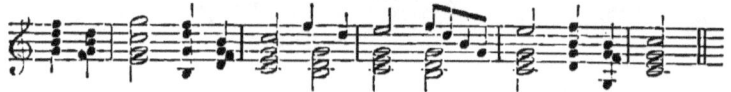

This is a signal distinction from all prepared discords, which can have no preparation but in the part wherein they are first presented, and which must invariably be resolved in that one same part.

M.—CHAP. X. SECT. 12.—There are exceptions from the diatonic rule in the treatment of the chord of the dominant 7th, as regards the chord to which it proceeds, and as regards also the notes on which its discordant intervals are resolved. It may be resolved on an inversion of the chord of the subdominant—

or upon a chromatic supertonic discord—

or upon a chromatic tonic discord—

Similar exceptional resolutions are made of the chords of the dominant minor 9th (Chap. XI. sect. 26), the dominant major 9th (Chap. XI. sect. 36), the dominant minor 13th (Chap. XIII. sect. 9), and the dominant major 13th (Chap. XIII. sect. 19), provided, in all cases, the rules for the progression of the imperfect intervals be fulfilled (Chap. XV. sect. 8).

N.—CHAP. X. SECT. 30.—This chord may be resolved upon the chord of the subdominant without necessitating modulation, provided the chords immediately following such resolution be characteristic of the primary key; but then the whole phrase must be regarded, rather than the two chords, as maintaining the original tonality :—

A proof that the key is not disestablished by this resolution, is, its satisfactory effect when occurring upon a dominant pedal :—

Similar resolution is made, with like integrity to the key, of the chords of the tonic minor 9th (Chap. XI. sect. 54), the tonic major 9th (Chap. XI. sect. 59), the tonic minor 13th (Chap. XIII. sect. 29), and the tonic major 13th (Chap. XIII. sect. 35).

O.—Progressive Exercises, p. 77, precede all other examples of chords of the 7th in the minor key by an example of the 7th on the key-note, which, like that on the subdominant, can only be used in the last inversion :—

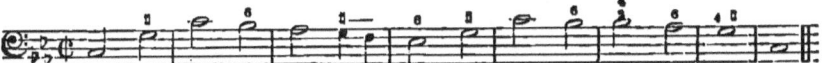

P.—Progressive Exercises, p. 81, precede all other examples of chords of the 9th in the minor key by an example of the 9th and 7th on the key-note, which can only be used in the third inversion :—

Insert also an example of the 9th and 7th on the subdominant, which, likewise, is only available in the third inversion :—

Q.—Chap. V. Sect. 2.—During a pedal, the key may change from that in which the pedal-note is dominant to that in which it is tonic, or from that in which the pedal-note is tonic to that in which it is dominant. The double or pedal of tonic and dominant may be employed if the tonic be the lower note, but then the one key must prevail throughout its continuance.

R.—Chap. XIV. Sects. 2 and 7.—The dominant generates the supertonic as the third sound in its harmonic series, and the continuation of this series includes the major 3rd of

O

the supertonic. The tonic and dominant stand in the same harmonic relationship as the dominant and supertonic. Hence the dominant and tonic, respectively, are the roots of the chords of augmented 6th on the minor 6th and minor 2nd of the key.

S.—CHAP. XI. SECT. 20.—When the root and 3rd are omitted, the 7th and 9th cease to be discords, and are therefore free in their progression, as is the entire chord. The chord is then identical with the first inversion on the 4th of the minor key. (Chap. IV. sect. 2).

T.—CHAP. XII. SECT. 5.—If the root be omitted, the chord thus resolved resembles the chord of the 7th with diminished 5th on the 2nd of the minor key (Chap. X. sect. 9), but differs from this in not needing preparation of its dissonant notes.

U.—CHAP. IV. SECT. 32.—This chord may proceed to the chord of the dominant, without necessitating modulation, provided the chords immediately following such resolution be characteristic of the primary key; but then the whole phrase must be regarded, rather than the two chords, as maintaining the original tonality.

V.—The major 6th of the key is rarely available in a minor key, except in the chromatic concord of the supertonic, or the chords of the 7th (Chap. X. sect. 21), and the 9th (Chap. XI. sect. 38) that are derived from the same root. It is, however, sometimes used as the major 3rd of the subdominant, but then is approached and quitted by a descending semitone. The major 3rd in the chord of the key-note is occasionally used in the minor key under the same conditions as the major 3rd of the subdominant.

W.—SUPERTONIC MAJOR THIRTEENTH.—A chord of the major 13th on the supertonic may be taken without preparation in both the major and minor key. The major 13th may be resolved on the 5th of the same chord if the 13th be accompanied with the 7th; but if the 7th be omitted, the root must proceed to the 7th when the 13th goes to the 5th.

The 13th may be resolved on the 7th, and then may or may not be accompanied with the 5th.

If resolved on a chord derived from another root, the 13th may remain to be the 3rd of the dominant, but then must not be accompanied with the 7th.

It may also proceed by chromatic semitone to the 7th of the tonic.

₊ *The foregoing instances may be used in the several inversions.*

X.—Chap. VIII., sect. 5.—Though the chord continue till the suspension be resolved, either the bass or any other part may proceed by leap or through passing-notes from one to another note of the chord, provided such moving part approach not by similar motion the note or the 8th of the note on which the suspension is resolved.

Y.—Chap. XI., sect. 7.—In the inversions of the mediant chord of the 9th in the major key, and of the supertonic and mediant chords of the 9th in the minor key, the root being omitted, the 5th ceases to be dissonant, and therefore needs no preparation. (Chap. XI. sect. 11.)

Z.—Chap. VIII., sect. 4.—The effect of consecutive 5ths is evaded if the 5th of the chord rise to the root, or either fall or rise to the 3rd, when the inverted 9th proceeds to the root.

AA.—CHAP. III. SECT. 15.—A discordant note may not be doubled, except when it is repeated as a concord in the following harmony. (Chap. X. Sect. 25.)

BB.—Chap. IV. Sect. 13.—Recommendation : When in a minor key, the chords of the dominant and submediant occur in succession, whichever precedes the other, it is expedient to have no 8th to the bass in the submediant chord, but to double the 3rd in the same :—

CC.—Chap. VIII. Sect. 14.—The diminished 5th on the supertonic of the minor key also is dissonant, but cannot be used as a suspension because its resolution upward would be by step of an augmented 2nd.   (Chap. III. Sect. 2.)

DD.—Chap. X. Sects. 24 and 25.—The chord of the dominant 7th may be resolved on an inversion of the chord of the subdominant, when the treatment of the 7th is the same as of that in the chord of the supertonic 7th when this is resolved on an inversion of the chord of the key-note.

EE.—Chap. IV. Sect. 20.—Less objectionable, but still undesirable, is the doubling of the bass when it is the minor 3rd of a chord, except only in the first inversion of the triad of the mediant. In the first inversion of a diminished triad (Chap. IV. Sects. 17, 21, and 22) the bass may freely be doubled.